Weeping for Raven
Inducing the Calm

BOOK I

Mel L. Kinder

Black Rose Writing

www.blackrosewriting.com

The final approval for this literary material is granted by the author.

First printing

All characters appearing in this work are fictitious. Any resemblance to real persons, living or dead, is purely coincidental.

ISBN: 978-1-61296-052-4

PUBLISHED BY BLACK ROSE WRITING

www.blackrosewriting.com

Printed in the United States of America

Weeping for Raven is printed in Byington

In loving memory of Virginia Mary "Kadamus" Trionfi (Metal Grandma).

I am forever grateful for your wisdom.

Acknowledgments

My husband John for your loving encouragement and participation in cover design ideas, my 'sister-like' best friend Chanetta for encouraging me when things got rough and proofing all of my drafts, my cousin Heather for bringing the raven-rose concept to life on paper, my parents for encouraging my life-long gift-of-gab, my cousin Ray for inspiring me to do whatever my heart desires no matter how crazy, Michael for lending me his eyes for cover design ideas, Erin Krey for the brief once-over of my manuscript, Black Rose Writing for giving me the opportunity to share my vision with the world, and everyone who left feedback about my sample pages via my website, all of my friends—four-legged included—at Camp Bow-Wow Brighton.

Weeping for Raven
Inducing the Calm

BOOK I

Preface

She opened her eyes to find the bright blue sky staring back at her. Not the baby-blue sky she would have expected—had she expected to wake up outdoors at all—more of a turquoise and aqua blend. She blinked a few times and stared to make sense of it all. *Why am I outside? I should be in my bed,* she wondered while rolling to one side. She pushed herself up from the ground feeling wobbly and disoriented. Gathering her senses she observed her surroundings—a garden of plants, flowers, and trees.

Did I die in my sleep? Her body felt strange, as if violently vibrated—like driving over rumble strips on the freeway. Waving her arms she tried to shake off the uncomfortable sensation.

Did I sleepwalk to this place? She turned to look behind herself. There stood a cottage-style house about half of an acre away. *Everything is too perfect,* her mind instantly protested. The blend of subtle complimentary natural fragrances were unquestionably breathtaking.

Ah—I must be dreaming. If I were dreaming would I know? She thought about pinching herself to see if it were a dream. *That is absurd. So what then? Flap my arms and attempt to fly? That is even more absurd.* She wondered if it were possible to think rationally or be self-conscious while dreaming.

A light warm breeze brushed against her face lightly ruffling her hair. Instinctively, she closed her eyes, took a deep breath and ran her fingers through her hair to brush it back away from her face. "My hair!" She took a strand between her fingers and pulled it forward. "Red! And curly!" Letting the strand fall from her fingers, it sprang into a large curl. "Beautiful, but not mine," she said aloud thinking, *now I know I'm dreaming!*

A buzzing sound in her head grew louder as her surroundings began to tilt out of control. She could no longer feel the lower half of her body. Everything began to turn sideways and then went blurry before fading to black.

Fluctuating between conscious and unconscious was disorienting. She felt as if her body were floating, paired with a subtle swaying sensation. A light breeze brushed past her face, which felt so good she could barely hold her grip on consciousness. A subtle whizzing sound—soothing like road noise—passed her ears. The source of the soothing breeze, was his fast, yet graceful, retreat back to the car with her in his arms. She sank into the depths again.

Chapter One

Gwen followed the arrows on the wall in search of the counselor's office. Rounding the corner she saw a row of chairs against the wall—mostly full of students. She signed in and took the only seat available. The boy to her right was sketching something on a blank, unlined pad of paper. The girl to her left was flipping through the catalog for the upcoming semester.

Crap! I forgot to grab a catalog. What am I gonna do while I wait? Knowing she would make no decisions without a counselor anyway she thought, *I guess there's no point in reading the catalog; other than to look busy.* Then she remembered her cell phone came equipped with games.

Out of the three games, she chose to pop colored bubbles. This occupied much more time than she thought it would. A few hours passed before she quit playing the game. Her eyes felt dry and strained. *Well, that sucked up some battery-life!* She looked around to see that some of the students who had formed a line were now occupying various seats where others had been called into the office. The young artist was still sketching beside her. Gwen didn't want to seem rude or nosy but was so amazed by his skill. What started out as line-after-line in different directions had transformed into a castle on a breathtaking landscape. "Amazing!" Gwen said just above a whisper. She could not help but watch him work now.

The pencil slowed then came to a stop. He looked at

her with his muddy green eyes.

"Uh—I—didn't mean to be nosy—it's just—I saw out of the corner of my eye—and wow!" Her words came out in a cluster of stumbles.

The boy smiled and shook his head looking back down at his work. He spoke quietly as he started adding lines—the finishing touches to his work. "I've got to do *something* to pass the time." Eying the phone in her had he asked, "What time is it anyway?"

Gwen hit the button to light up the screen. "It's 8:00."

"Wow. Four hours. It doesn't look like they are going to call me in anytime soon. Most of these people were already here when I sat down." The boy wasn't as disappointed as he attempted to sound.

"Have you been working on this drawing the entire time?" Gwen looked shocked though not surprised given the superior detail of the sketch.

"Yeah. I guess I have." He raised his eyebrows, put his pencil down, and reached his hand out to introduce himself, "I'm Mimic."

"Mimic? Like as in to mimic someone?" Gwen felt stupid for asking, though she was sure it was a justifiable question.

"I grew up with a stutter. My name is Mick but it always came out sounding like Mimic whenever I introduced myself, hence the nick-name," he recollected, "I guess it grew on me."

"You weren't offended?" Gwen asked curiously.

He breathed out a sigh and stared through the brick wall across the hallway, "No. I can't blame others for what they don't understand. I was unique and amusing to them," he shrugged it off, "Whatever."

"You don't stutter now." Gwen stated like fact. His maturity and calm demeanor impressed her. Mimic's story upset her even though she didn't know him.

4

"When I get overly nervous or excited it happens. When my mind and mouth are in a race with one another." He shook off the topic, "So what's your story?"

"My story," Gwen smiled, "it's more like a novella." She waited for him to smile back in acknowledgment. "I'm Gwen. I've lived in the area my whole life and I'm not sure what to major in. I hope a counselor can help me figure that out." She paused and redirected the focus on him. "So Mimic? What's your major? Maybe we'll have a class together and we can avoid that whole first-day-of-not-knowing-anybody thing."

"I'm taking Art and Design. I'm sure we have some of the same general studies class requirements." Mimic said sounding surprised and definitely interested in the idea of taking classes together. He wasn't used to girls initiating conversation with him, if they acknowledged his presence at all. What Mimic did not know was that Gwen had the same problem. For Gwen, it was more of a preference. Still healing the wounds of losing her best friend Baylee—a few years prior—Gwen wasn't sure if she would ever let anyone get close to her again.

"I have been considering photography or something in the film industry, like on the editing side or something," Gwen replied. "I like to paint and draw," she added.

Gwen and Mimic thumbed through a course catalog, which he had stashed underneath the sketch pad. They compared their general study prerequisites and planned to take whatever classes together they could. This was equally exciting for both of them as neither one had many friends. The time they spent together talking, outside of the counselor's office, made minutes feel like seconds. They were no longer aware of their surroundings, which caused Mick to let his name slip passed him when called.

"Mick, I think they are calling you in now. Is your last name Thompson?"

"Yep. That's me. It was great meeting you. Hope to see ya around." He gave her one last look and with a smile she wouldn't soon forget. It felt like the last time she would see him, though she truly hoped it would not be.

"Grandma! Grandpa! I'm home!" Gwen called as she entered the front door, using the toe of one sneaker to push the heel of the other sneaker off, then using the toe of her sock to push off the other sneaker. *I'm so ready to throw down on some chow.* Her curiosities about Mimic drowned out by the sound of her growling belly. *A six-hour wait for a half hour discussion. Stupid.*

The smell of Grandma Penn's homemade spaghetti sauce filled the air. Always a good sign that Beverly, a.k.a. Grandma, was in an exceptionally good mood. Bev always seemed happy to the outside world, but it only seemed that way. She constantly mourned the mental health of her daughter—Gwen's mother—Madison.

Gwen announced her arrival before proceeding further into the house, a habit formed in her youth. Sometimes her grandparents argued about her mother behind her back. Overwhelmed by guilt for burdening her grandparents, she tried to give them the privacy they deserve.

Bev stood stirring the pot of steaming hot spaghetti sauce. "Oh dear, you are home just in time. I was afraid I was going to have to simmer this sauce a little longer. It's just right."

"Smells awesome! I'm so hungry right now. Where is Grandpa?" Gwen asked curiously.

"He's out in the garage again. Trying to get that old

boat motor going. I don't know why he doesn't just buy a new motor for that thing. It's as old as the hills and surely other parts are ready to go. You know Pa, he insists on fixing everything himself." Bev half-smiled.

Benjamin Penn was old-fashioned; he liked to get his hands dirty. This was one of the characteristics Bev fell in love with many years ago. They were old, but young romantics at heart. Gwen hoped someday she could find such a companion. Gwen thought of herself as a realist; she didn't waste time with her head in the clouds. So many girls she knew were so obsessed with finding prince charming that it interfered with their logical thought processes.

Gwen took a seat in her usual place at the dinner table.

"Pa! Come on now, dinner's done," Bev yelled out the door toward the garage.

Gwen heard Ben's muffled voice yelled back in the distance. "Gwen home?"

"Yeah. She's here. We're waiting on you," Bev yelled back, then let the screen door shut itself; returning to the stove to stir the sauce. Gwen noticed the noodles were fully cooked and set aside to cool. Her belly rumbled again.

Grandpa Penn was not far behind the closing screen door. *I bet he is starving too,* Gwen thought. Once Ben got into a project, he was in deep; hard to pull away from a project no matter how small its significance. He liked to *Git'r done,* as *Larry the Cable Guy* would say.

"Evening hon." Ben kissed Gwen on top of her head. He refrained from touching anything in the house; his hands were covered in filth.

"Hey Grandpa," Gwen replied before he left the room. Ben hurried to the restroom to wash his hands, and likely take care of any other natural human processes postponed while working on his boat. Gwen was the same way when into a good book.

Eating at the dinner table was a tradition the Penn family held onto. Although most families these days piled their plates and sat in front of their large flat-screen television sets, the Penn's treasured this family time together. Gwen was not a big fan of television anyway, Bev rather read books and do arts and crafts, and Ben enjoyed the great outdoors. Not in the way a hunter does. Ben was a fan of living things, preferably the kind that didn't speak. He wasn't a grumpy old man by any means, just not much of a people-person. Biting his tongue to spare others' feelings was far from his favorite pastime.

Bev loved animals, and the company of others. She believed smiling had the power to cure to all of the world's problems. *"A smile can save a life,"* Gwen heard it her whole life. Gwen wished she could live with such feelings of hope, but found herself to be a fairly equal divide among her grandparents. She wanted to believe in the good of mankind, but in the days of school shootings and Wallstreet suicides, holding onto that belief felt like believing in Santa Clause or the Tooth Fairy.

"How did your meet with the counselor go?" Ben asked while wiping his chin with a napkin.

"Great. It's a nice school and I'm excited" she said. "College—wow." Gwen wasn't as excited as she attempted to sound.

Bev finished chewing a mouthful before asking, "Schoolcraft dear? Are you sure you don't want to go to one of those fancy universities? I saw the letters and postcards in the mail. I know this isn't your only option?" Bev's concern was obvious; that Gwen may feel obligated to stay close to home. Bev refrained from asking about her plans to go to the art university—suspecting she knew why Gwen's plans changed. Bev had not been born without mother's intuition. Gwen assumed grandmother's intuition was like x-ray vision.

"I'm totally sure Grandma. I don't need to go to an expensive school. Schoolcraft has plenty of transfer programs and if I don't like it there, I'll just go to a different community college. I want to stay close to home," Gwen explained.

Bev sighed and shifted her glance to Ben as if to say *I told you so.*

Ben rolled his eyes at Bev—knowing she wouldn't take it to heart. They had years of experience communicating silently.

"What?" Gwen asked. "I want this," she reaffirmed and added, "I couldn't stand it if something happened to either of you and I wasn't nearby. I couldn't live with myself!"

Ben lost the bet with Bev, therefore it was his turn to speak. "Look hon, we love that you are concerned for our safety, but we don't want to hold you back. You deserve the room to spread your wings and show your colors. You don't have to worry about us old folks. We've survived this long."

Truth was, Ben was tickled pink on the inside that Gwen decided to stay close to home. He wasn't ready to lose his little girl just yet. The time would come to let her go and he wouldn't stand in her way, but this did make it hard for him to give the encouragement speech. While encouraging Gwen to stay home, he was secretly praying that she would argue with him. Though he hated confrontation, this was a battle he wanted to lose.

"I am sure about this. Unless you want to be rid of me. I totally understand if you want more space. I can find a place if you..."

"No!" Ben interrupted. He hadn't meant to sound so demanding but he definitely wasn't ready for her to move out of the house. Ben closed his eyes, sighed and began again, "I mean, if that is what you want—but that is not what we are trying to say. We're just worried that you might be making this decision for the wrong reasons. We will support you in whatever you choose."

"I know that," Gwen said. "I'm not really sure which path I want to pursue yet, so this is the best option. I will take the basic classes required and then once I figure out what I want to do, I'll transfer to a four-year university. I think it's a win-win situation for all of us," Gwen said in an upbeat and convincing tone.

"That sounds like a good plan," Ben replied while raising an eyebrow at Bev.

"Are you guys playing mind-chess again?" Gwen asked jokingly. They both smiled at her. "Should I ask who is winning?" Gwen asked.

They chuckled but said nothing more about it. She figured they kept a secret tally board somewhere in their bedroom to keep an ongoing score behind her back. She imagined an even score.

Gwen entered her bedroom feeling sleepy, but not tired enough to fall asleep. She visually scanned the room for the new book she was reading. At first she saw nothing. Then an idea popped into her head. Whinny: the big orange, tan, and cream colored cross-eyed cat who had a built-in intuition about laying on, or sitting on, whatever currently most held Gwen's attention. She spotted her furry friend across the room. Whinny stood and began to stretch his back. His tail hooked like an old man's cane standing on end. Gwen extended her hand inviting Whinny to rub his forehead against her forearm. Pushing his cheek across her sleeve he proceeded to rub the side of his body too—sporting a closed-eyed grin of appreciation.

"Just as I suspected," she said recognizing the book cover peaking out from where her large orange cat stood begging for attention.

Instead of grabbing the book, Gwen opted to pick Whinny up instead. Whinny had been waiting for this moment all day. Scooping his back up onto her forearm she flipped him like a baby in her arms—Whinny's favorite embrace. He stretched and pressed his neck against her forearm so he could get a better perspective of his, now, upside-down surroundings. His front legs stuck straight up in the air, back legs stretched out straight as a board. Gwen felt his purr rumbling in her chest. She slowly walked Whinny around the room, allowing him to get his fix before sitting on the edge of her bed where she lay him down next to her. He didn't hesitate to climb up onto her hip and then walk up to her chest where he stood purring and massaging his heavy paws into her chest—which felt like broomsticks poking her. She winced at the weight beneath each foot as he shifted it between his front legs. *Why does he always do this?* she wondered. She waited for him to lay on her chest before petting him again—not encouraging him to stand any longer. She drew in a deep sigh and let her mind run on autopilot.

Thinking of college quickly led to thinking about Mimic; focusing on his sweet characteristics rather than any defining physical feature. She liked something about him and wasn't really sure what it was. It wasn't physical attraction, though his muddy green eyes were pretty. Gwen distrusted the physically attractive. *Cute is trouble,* was her motto. Mimic was cute in his own way; not the dangerous way.

11

"You are just as cute as can be! And I know you are trouble mister," Gwen said as she scratched Whinny's head in sync with her accusation. Whinny squeezed his eyes closed and smiled his cat-grin. He didn't care what Gwen was saying—but it felt darn good.

Though a fan of the concept of love, Gwen believed it was only meant for some. She believed it was more of a miracle; happening only to a select few. Love and romance must exist—her grandparents were proof of that. Something about the way they looked at each other—the sort of thing you read about and heard about in fairy tales. To Gwen, love seemed more like a dangerous drug; one could lose their mind in it. *People do really stupid things in the name of love. People do really stupid things in the name of religion. Heck, people just love to do really stupid things for any justifiable cause. People, are just plain stupid.*

"Not me Whinny. I've got you, Grandma, and Grandpa. That's all I need. I'm not waiting around for some fairy tale to sweep me off my feet," Gwen said scratching Whinny's chin. Whinny extended his chin out offering a better reach. "My little prince charming," Gwen said pushing Whinny's ears back to plant a kiss on his head before picking him up, and placing him aside. Gwen retrieved the book she had been searching for and plopped it on the bed. *Nothing like a nice warm shower, fresh linens, and a good book,* she thought. *I wonder if Whinny will curl up on the bed as usual, or if he will make another attempt to hide my book.*

Chapter Two

What started out as an ordinary Thursday for Rook Dresden turned out to be anything but ordinary; the first link in a chain of unforeseeable, life-altering events.

Every Thursday, Rook visited his younger sister Raven, at the hospital. Sharing his weekly stories as an auto-mechanic as if it were a thrilling and adventurous journey. The medical machines had been her guardian angels for just over two years, but Rook's faith in her recovery has never wavered. The routine was effortless—he functioned on autopilot—with the exception of this day. He was almost to the hospital when he realized he forgot his guitar. Beating himself up over such an oversight, "I must be losing my mind," he thought turning the car around to backtrack.

Though he was in and out of the house quickly, in the time it took to get back on the road, something caused traffic to halt. "This back-up must go on for a mile," he complained aloud. "What the heck is going on today?" It felt like everything was going against his grain. He took a deep breath and turned down the nearest side-road. He was not going to let a few obstacles rattle his nerves today. *I will be in a Zen mood for Raven.*

Rook never ventured this side-road before but was sure he could navigate just fine with his phenomenal sense of direction. Passing many open fields and flowering trees he spotted a figure in the distance—a female figure facing the opposite direction. Large red curls blew in the breeze along with the olive green dress she wore. The scene reminded him of an oil painting he reviewed in humanities class. He slowed the car watching her curiously, hoping she would turn around so he could see her face. Just when he thought she would turn around, she collapsed in the orchard.

Rook's heart sank to his stomach and before he knew it, he was flailing from the car to the girl—a good 150 feet to where she lay—yet he was there in seconds. He brushed the curls from her face and observed her porcelain features. Her eyes fluttered open and close. He scooped her up in his arms and ran for the car as fast as his legs would allow. Though the girl was weightless in his arms, he felt as though he were running in slow motion.

Gwen's eyelids were heavy. When she managed to force them up, they only rose half-way. Her body was still in sleep paralysis, or so she hoped. The first glimpse lasted only a second. She let her lids rest before attempting to open them again. When they opened fully they lasted only three seconds before snapping shut. Though her vision was blurry, she could tell she wasn't in her bedroom. Mumbling voices came into focus for the first time. She spent so much attention trying to open her eyes that she had not noticed the sounds around her until now. She rested her lids again. The curiosity began to eat away at her. Using the anxiety to push her lids open again her eyes began to focus and she could see a face. The eyes caught and held her attention—the way a glittery toy held a baby's.

His eyes, the irises, back-lit gray; gray clouds behind transparent glass, with darker reflective silver lines like thin metallic fibers throughout, sun-bursting around his deep black pupils. Behind his irises resembled a gray curtain with silver threads woven in, draped over a lampshade illuminated by a dimly lit light-bulb—as if his piercing bright eyes could see right down into her soul.

Oh no! I'm dead, she thought. Only an angel—certainly no mortal—could have such perfect features and serene eyes. Suddenly, she felt naked, insecure, and paralyzed for what seemed like an eternity—as if time stood still in that very moment. Though Gwen thought she was staring too much, for far too long she could not look away. *I must look like a deer caught in headlights!* She was sure that this was how a deer would feel. Gwen's eyelids remained open—closing them was the problem now. Gwen didn't want to close her eyes, she wanted to remember his face when she woke.

Rook turned his head, "She's awake!" he said with obvious excitement.

Gwen paid very close attention to the words he spoke. *"She's awake."* Gwen wondered if that meant she was not dead after-all. *I have never experienced death so perhaps this is the angel's lingo.*

Just then he was joined by another beautiful being. A darker complected woman with caramel and black spirals in her hair. She too had strange eyes, but her irises were bronze and copper toned. The copper outer rings and lines, which sunburst around her black pupils were shiny metallic like the silver threads in the man's eyes. The light bronze color backdrop resembled a dim light behind a mild sandy tan curtain. This tan backdrop translucent in comparison to the bold metallic copper lines.

I have never seen such beautiful eyes in my life! What is this place? Must be heaven, or a dream. The silver eyes were hypnotic and were so well complimented by his dark black hair with the midnight blue tint. The lady's copper-sandy eyes complimented her medium-brown complected, porcelain-smooth skin. Her hair color and texture perfectly suited her face. *They have to be angels or aliens. Maybe I was abducted from my bed like the stories you hear on the unsolved mysteries show.* If these beautiful beings were a figment of her imagination, she wanted to remember them with as much detail as possible so she could paint a picture when she woke. For now, Gwen accepted that she was dreaming rather than dead or abducted by aliens.

When either the lady or the man spoke, she heard two voices simultaneously. One, which seemed to be inside of her head, the other a physical sound; chiming in stereo. *I must have hit my head really hard when I fainted!* Gwen was so stunned that she couldn't listen to the words being spoken; only the strange stereo sound; like hearing sound for the first time. She tried to speak but her mouth was just as stubborn as her eye lids had been moments ago. *What the heck is wrong with me?* she wondered in frustration.

"Is she going to be alright?" Rook asked the nurse.

"I see no reason to suspect otherwise. She is in shock. Where did you say you found her?"

"I was on my way back here—I forgot my guitar," Rook recounted in his mind as he spoke, "I saw her standing in the distance, in an open field of flowers and trees. The way her dress and hair blew in the breeze..." Rook trailed off before continuing. "It was ironic and I couldn't help but slow down as I passed. She was facing away from me, so I wasn't worried about looking like a creep. Then she collapsed. I brought her here as fast as I could."

"Luckily you forgot that guitar. Who knows how long she would have been out there. Could you imagine if she would have woken after sunrise?"

After sunrise? I know it was daylight when I woke in the field. I remember the brilliant sky, Gwen thought.

"Yeah. Lucky." Rook's eyebrows dropped almost as fast as they rose. Gwen could tell he was finishing the sentence in his head rather than speaking it aloud.

She finally pried her eyes off the two angelic dream-beings to observe her surroundings. It resembled a hospital but there were no bright fluorescent lights overhead, just a large dome skylight over the bed. The colors in the room, though neutral, seemed intense; so dense and rich. Even the most drab of colors were beautiful. Gwen felt like a newborn child seeing objects for the first time. She always appreciated natural beauty but this nature was insanely beautiful.

Her senses were overwhelmed; exhausted. *How could I be sleepy while dreaming? I wonder what I'll wake up to next.* She rolled her mind's eye at the thought. *What if I never see him again?* Gwen acknowledged the sudden heaviness in her center. *Why do I even care? He's not real, get over it!* Gwen was sure she knew the answer to the last question but wished it wasn't true. *Pathetic—Gwen—Pathetic.* Her eyes drifted back to sleep.

"What do you think?" Rook asked the nurse.

"I only detected minor bumps, indicating no major head trauma and her eyes are responding the way they should. The answer to the question which, I think, you really mean to ask is, "will she reawaken tonight?" and the answer is, "highly unlikely.""

Rook smiled. The nurses at the hospital knew he had a genuine care for people. They joked that he should have been a nurse. As much as Rook loved people, he loved machines more. They were less complicated, easier to reason with, could be repaired and even live forever.

"I'll take that as a hint and be on my way. I've got one

more stop to make before I head out."

The nurse smiled and nodded. She knew his Thursday evening routine—all of the staff did.

Feeling herself regain consciousness Gwen decided to keep her eyes closed for a moment longer to envision the highlights of the bizarre dream. She opened her eyes and saw that nothing changed. *I'm still in the hospital!* She sat up and looked around the room anxious; her heart began to thump harder in her chest. The air felt thinner and she was suddenly dizzy. She laid back down looking up at the ceiling as if to find the answer scribbled there in the dome skylight.

Yesterday, I thought I was dreaming. Today I don't know what to think. I'm so confused! I'm losing my mind! That's it. My mother is crazy and I inherited her insanity! As if she needed one more reason to hate her.

The door cracked open and startled Gwen out of deep contemplation.

"Good morning! You look good and alert today," the nurse greeted enthusiastically. The nurse: the darker-complected, two-toned hair beauty-queen, with the stunning copper and sand colored eyes. The nurses voice still resonated with the strange stereo tone as before.

Gwen attempted to speak her first words since waking, "Good... morning." She listened to her own words as she spoke them and was stunned by the sound that escaped her lips; not a voice she recognized. She scooted her butt back and propped her back up against the layer of pillows behind her.

"Do you remember anything?" the nurse asked compassionately.

Gwen thought about waking in the flowers. "No. Not... really. I'm not sure where... I am, or how... I got here."

"You have a few minor bumps on your head but it's nothing serious. How do you feel? Any headache or neck pain?" The nurse shined a green light in Gwen's eyes.

"No. I'm a little dizzy and pretty confused. My hearing is funny and everything looks brighter than usual."

"Hmm..." The nurse seemed to disregard the symptoms as if insignificant. Gwen was irritated by medical practitioners who overlooked symptoms, which she thought were relevant. *I am no doctor, but I know my own body well enough to know when something isn't right. I definitely don't feel like myself.*

"Who was that guy? The one who was here yesterday?" This question concerned her the most, even though she would deny it to the death. Gwen was never boy-crazy by any means, but this one particular guy was so unreal, and intriguing that she couldn't help it. *Who in their right mind could?* Gwen justified.

"Only the man whom, most likely, saved your life. I can't think of his name off-hand, but he is a regular here."

"Does he work here?" Her interest more obvious with each question. A smile crept on the nurses face as she tried to maintain a professional but courteous persona.

"No. He is a regular visitor. Has been for a while now. Thursdays I think. Yesterday was Thursday right?" She quickly answered her own question, "Yep, Thursdays," she confirmed with a nod and a smile. "A genuine sweetheart, that one." The nurse winked and smiled.

Gwen felt as if she were beginning to blush, butterflies flapped chaotically in her stomach. *Get a grip! Relax! Gees. These teeny-bopper crushes are so beneath me!* Gwen refused to allow herself to fall victim to such nonsense. Girls who fell into that crap were mindless and weak. Gwen vowed to never fall victim to such nonsensical behavior over some guy. No one would have power over her, in any way, if she could help it. Those who stole your heart could steal your mind and ruin your life. She saw it time-and-time again in high school. Most of those girls wind up pregnant and alone. One girl even committed suicide over some schmuck who promised to love her forever. Turns out he just used her to get close to her younger, hotter, cousin. Back-stabbing cousin was a fool just the same. Gwen always wondered what it was that led girls, and even, grown women to such foolishness. Even the smartest of them fell into some of the most basic traps. It all seemed so obvious to her.

Gwen laid back down and pulled in a deep sigh of fresh, fragrant air of the surrounding plants and blossoms. She began to worry about her grandparents. *Where do they think I am?*

The nurse re-entered the room with an armful of fresh linens. She continued her side of the conversation, as if she never left the room. "In fact, I would not be surprised if your guy friend comes back here today to check on you."

Gwen hid her excitement but could not contain the smile that crept out. *Don't hold your breath Gwen,* her inner-voice spoke in the back of her mind—reminding her how pointless it was to have such hopes. *It's my delusion. I should enjoy it while it lasts,* she argued with herself.

"When will I be able to move about freely?" Gwen knew she would become stir-crazy and soon. Her curiosity grew with each passing hour.

"You are free to leave any time. But you're welcome to stay as long as you like," the nurse reminded her.

Yeah I bet, the longer I stay, the more money they get right? The nurse sounded sincere enough but Gwen learned a long time ago that nothing comes without a price, even compassion, or the illusion of honesty.

Gwen tried to remember his face and the sound of his voice. The thoughts calmed her and she fell asleep. Sleep was a good way to pass the time right now; comforting in one way, but nerve-racking in another. Every time she woke —every few hours—she expected to see her bedroom and when she did not, she worried.

What am I going to do? I can't stay here forever. They will never find me here; wherever here is. Just as Gwen was beginning to feel hopeless her mood suddenly changed when she heard his voice outside of her room. As if she could feel it and hear it. She sat up in the bed and ran her fingers through her hair like a comb. His voice resonated around her solar plexus, a sort of energy; a sensation that felt as if something were pulling her from the inside out. It didn't hurt, but it was disorienting.

The door opened and she saw him again; this time she was fully alert and awake. His style of dress unique; clean, neat, but different. His hair was unique as well—shiny black, a hint of blue in the light. *Very abstract for lack of a better word. It looks like he stuck his head in wood-chipper and then went from there. Not messy, kind of artistic. I wonder how he came up with this look. I wonder if he came up with it or if he just let some hair dresser experiment. What is the name for this sort of style? Not punk-rock. Something with an E. Emo! Right! The first time I heard the term it reminded me of Elmo.* Gwen was so taken by his appearance that her ears heard his voice but her brain refused to translate. She was dazed and deep in thought. *I wonder if his eyes glow in the dark like cats.* Her memory of his eyes had done them no justice.

The pulling in her center spiraled outward more intensely. She felt all of her worries drift away as she looked into his eyes. She was captivated; his gaze had locked hers in place. *Unbelievable! I must have been too weak yesterday to feel this, whatever this is. Not completely unpleasant. It sort-of tickles. Like driving fast over a hill.* The sensation was like an itch in the way of persistence. To Gwen it felt like a thirst she didn't know how to quench.

"Good to see you awake. How are you feeling?" He took a seat in the guest sofa against the wall between two windows.

"I uh—feel..." she searched for the words and looked as confused as she felt.

He smiled and waited patiently for her to piece her thoughts together. "The nurse says you seem to be in pretty good shape. Would you like to go for a walk or something? Get out and get some fresh air, maybe a change of scenery? You must be going nuts by now, just hanging out in this place all morning."

"It's only been one day. Hasn't it?" Gwen stated and then wondered.

"So I'm wrong? You aren't ready to get out of here?"

"I don't know what I want, where I'll go or even where I am," she answered.

"Amnesia?" Rook asked.

"I don't think that's it. I think I might be losing my mind or something." After she said it she felt like an idiot. *Just the sort of thing to say to impress a guy. Way to go Gwen!* "I've been getting the feeling like—I should get out of here soon. I'm not sure why and like I said, I don't know where to go."

He assumed that the girl with the fiery red hair didn't even know her own name so he spared the introduction. He didn't want to be rude. "I can take you back to the orchard where I found you, if you like. Maybe it will bring back some memories. If not, we can always come back here. I have to come back today anyway."

The thought of spending time alone with him away from this place was an offer she could hardly resist. *If he were going to do something to me, he would have done it while I was unconscious in the field.* He didn't strike Gwen as the serial killer type, but if she were sure of anything it was that cute is trouble. Cute got people into trouble. Partly to blame for over occupancy at the animal shelters. It weakened good judgment. *Not all serial killers are unattractive,* she reminded herself. Cute is the wild-card that offers an advantage to the one who has it in their possession. They still have to know how to play the game and that is something Gwen felt good about. She was sure she had heard of, seen or thought of, every possible trick in the book. Gwen was leery of beautiful things and beautiful people. "Okay." She cringed at the over-enthusiastic and unfamiliar tone of her voice—much louder and bolder than she expected. He didn't seem to notice.

Chapter Three

The parking lot was fairly empty. The colorful brilliance brought back the short memory of the orchard. "Amazing!" Rook detected a sort of satisfaction in her reaction to the outdoors. "You've only been in for one day. You act like you've been locked away for months!" Rook chuckled.

"I *feel* like I've been locked away for months. I feel like running wild. I don't know what's happening to me. The feeling is indescribable. I can't remember ever feeling so excited, energetic, and clueless at the same time!" *Did the nurse drug me?* Gwen wondered.

"Well, if you're this excited about the hospital parking lot just wait until you see the orchard," Rook chuckled.

Gwen found herself easily distracted by the deep green of the grass and the contrasting purple flowers that speckled the ground. So distracted that she failed to notice the cars had no tires nor headlights. When she did finally observe the few surrounding vehicles, she was perplexed by the missing tires. *Are they sunk into those plastic pad things? They hardly even resemble cars. Dreaming...* Gwen reminded herself.

"This is my ride," Rook said with pride.

Wow! The most richest blue and the deepest black I have ever seen. Her expression said it all. Rook felt his ego inflate.

Gwen approached the passenger side of the blue & black car and was startled by the reflection in the dark tinted glass. She saw the ghost of a beautiful woman looking back at her from inside of the car. Gwen recognized the curls and noticed that the ghost's expressions changed in sync with her own.

"Wow! You really do like this car huh?" Rook laughed as he watched her stare in awe.

She didn't have time to observe the transparent image in the glass. *Oh crap! Gwen act natural. Otherwise he might bring you back to a different sort of hospital,* her inner-voice warned.

No door handle! Great! Now what? A cold sensation of panic washed over her. Rook placed his palm down on the passenger side door and it popped open. *Gentleman; of course,* she thought sarcastically. *I wonder if all of my dreamworld cars have this as a standard feature, or if it's his own personal custom touch. Well, no need to worry about having his car stolen with this nifty little feature.*

Gwen wanted to pull down the visor and pretend to check her hair or makeup—some excuse to get a better look at herself—but there was no visor on either side.

They strapped themselves in. Gwen watched Rook, like a learning child, as he put his hand around what appeared to be a shift lever. Light formed around his fingertips. Rook released the lever leaving behind his hand-print traced out with blue-white light on the black rubber lever. She saw no markings to indicate park, neutral, reverse, etc.

Holy crap! The car is lifting. Is it floating? Maybe it's just the tires coming up out of that plastic-looking parking pad.

The car lifted and began turning effortlessly; a completely smooth transition. *No sound! Where the heck is the ignition for this thing?* Gwen was glad that his attention was on the road and not on her as she tried to keep her jaw from falling open. *No road noise. We are flying!* Gwen held her excitement inside the best she could but was sure she left some on her expression. The car flew just above the road.

25

Gwen tried desperately not to panic. *Just a dream. It's just a dream. Everything will be fine.* Rook's attention focused on her now. "Why so quiet?" he asked curiously.

Gwen shifted in her seat and looked out the window. *I don't think I can lie to him while making eye contact. He just might hypnotize the truth right out of me and then off to the loony bin we go!* "I was just thinking. Trying to figure things out in my head." Gwen paused to think of what else to say.

"Makes sense." Rook nodded. Gwen was glad that he accepted the answer with no further explanation. She could see he wanted to know more but was reluctant to ask. It made her feel mysterious. Perhaps if she were as mysterious to him, as he was to her, he would be just as compelled to be around her.

The car traveling 70 mph approached an intersection causing Gwen to panic and almost squeal before the car stopped effortlessly on its own. The ride was so smooth that she could have fallen asleep in the car—had it not been for all of the anxiety and excitement.

The car came to a calm stop in the driveway of a house, which reminded Gwen of her grandparent's house. She remembered seeing this house before fainting. Rook popped the car doors open. She got out and looked around to see if she could spot the place where she fainted.

"Well Red, this is it. Anything coming to mind?"

Gwen turned to look at him curiously. "Huh?"

"Do you recognize this place from yesterday?" He had not realized his pet-name for her slipped out.

"No. I got that? And the answer is maybe. What did you call me?"

He had been trying so hard to keep from putting her on the spot, or stressing her out.

Rook hoped he hadn't offended her. "Red. I uh—don't know your name and I wasn't sure if you remembered it or not. I didn't want to upset you."

Gwen laughed. She had forgotten about the red hair and the ghost in the tinted glass window. She was so wrapped up in the idea that she was dreaming that she didn't even think to ask him his name. "I'll tell you what I can. Don't worry about upsetting me. I am not upset at all. Actually, I'm having fun. Everything feels so new and exciting. I should pass out more often," she joked.

"Gwen," she offered her hand in introduction.

"Rook," he replied giving an uncertain one-eye glance at her unfamiliar gesture.

"Like the chess piece?" she asked pulling her hand back to her side reluctantly.

"Like the bird," he corrected.

She couldn't help but laugh. He gave her a confused glance ready to ask a question. Then she realized that he could have mistaken her amusement at the coincidence, as an insult.

She interrupted before Rook could speak, "It's just that... I was named after a bird too—sort of."

His eyes looked to the sky, eyebrows strained, lips twisted to one side, deeply contemplating before continuing, "I don't follow—I've never heard of a Gwen bird."

A detail she always hoped people would not piece together. She hated to have to tell him, but it was a little late for that now. *Walked yourself right into this one bigmouth!* "My last name is Penn." Gwen rolled her eyes slowly in an exaggerated motion as she spoke, looking at the ground shuffling dirt and pebbles around with her while anticipating his reaction. She didn't want to look him in the face just yet. Hoping to absorb less of the embarrassment. She braced herself for laughter and heckling, but he did neither. *Maybe he is slow to put it together.* She looked back up at him—he looked as if he were waiting for her to say something else.

"Penguin?" she added in a sarcastically charged tone.

"That *is* amusing," he replied while smirking.

"Embarrassing." Her eyes shifted back to the ground for a moment and then back to him.

"It's cute," he corrected. "A penguin is a bit more flattering than some ancient crow."

The compliment escalated the embarrassment causing her cheeks to ache and flush. She tried to imagine how much her new red hair would compliment her, now, red cheeks.

"Well the house looks familiar to me," Gwen said. It looked like a modified carbon-copy of her grandparent's house. The color scheme more neutral, the landscape breathtaking, the grass a deep forest green, the flowers a nice contrast to the lighter green plants—all strategically mixed in. A natural stone walkway to the front porch made from large stones—all just the right shape and size. She wondered how they were held together so nicely; no visible harsh lines or flaws in the construction. Small Japanese maples, and hostas, perfectly spaced surrounded by dark brown, almost black, fluffy, moist and healthy-looking dirt. No need for mulch. The purple and green colors popped against one another. *My grandparents landscape is nice but not nearly as grandiose!*

"I think I live here," Gwen said hesitantly.

"Do you think we should knock on the door?" she asked anxiously.

"Sure. What's the worst that could happen? If you don't

live here, maybe someone saw what happened or knows why you were out there."

Gwen knocked on the door and waited patiently. No one answered.

"Try the doorknob," Rook suggested.

Reluctantly, she put her hand on the door knob, then suddenly a glow of blue-white light appeared under her hand and fingers.

When she removed her hand from the door knob, she saw that her hand-print remained in the blue-white light, which faded when the door opened.

They looked at each other. "Well, it looks like you live here," Rook affirmed. "Ladies first." Rook gestured.

"Gee thanks." Gwen shot him a sarcastic glance.

"Hey, I'm just a guest here."

"I could be too for all I know," she countered.

Gwen took the initiative; taking the first steps inside, Rook followed. The room was more open and seemingly much larger than the Penn's house. No recliner, no television. Potted flowering trees in every corner of the large room. Two of which had slim, braided trunks; brilliantly colored flowers contrasting the pointy deep green leaves. The walls a subtle earthy tone. Colors Gwen would have chosen herself.

A large clock hung on the back wall where the television normally sat. It looked to be carved into an old tree; wrapped around it were antiqued shades of green, which resembled vines.

Two sofas sat facing one another with a rectangular glass table; decorative metal vines as its base, which sat long-sided in-between the sofas. On the short end of the table was a matching sofa chair. The furniture was set on, what appeared to be, a really expensive floor rug.

"Nice place you have here. Anything coming back yet?" Rook asked.

"Not really. I mean, it's familiar enough that I'm sure I know the floor-plan, but something is different. I don't remember this particular furniture, and things are not arranged the way I remember them." Gwen's face crumpled in concern—her features frozen like a statue.

Walking along slowly, observing the new version of her grandparent's house, she caught a glimpse out of the corner of her eye of an oval mirror framed in large pastel purple, lightly colored transparent shards of glass, alternating with darker, less translucent shards of a different size. She stopped in her tracks and stepped back to look in the mirror. She forgot about the new red hair, and already put the ghostly image on the tinted car window behind her. *I have got to see this. Me, with red curly hair!*

As she came into the mirror's line of sight, she moved slowly to acclimate to any impending shock. The bright, dark red wavy curls came into view and she knew that was the moment she would see herself clearly. Gwen eased her way into the view—like sticking a toe in a pool to check the temperature. When she finally came into view, she was not only shocked, but impressed. The shock turned to smugness as she checked out her perfect features with eyes silver like Rook's. *They really go good with my red hair and fair complexion.*

She had a hard time pulling herself away from the mirror. She wanted to examine everything: the shape of her nose and mouth, the spacing of her eyes, her perfectly arched manicured eyebrows. She wondered if he were as captivated by her beauty, as she was now. *A little wishful thinking perhaps,* Gwen thought, *Now I'm being egotistical.* It didn't feel that way—the reflection belonged to someone else. *Soon I will awaken, to see the same old plain face staring back at me: bland straight brown hair sticking up with pillow-imprints on the side of my face. Who cares if I've got an ego, this is my dream, my world, I can do whatever I want,* she

30

justified. Trying out a few different expressions and angles, she thought, *I don't even need makeup.*

Rook was browsing for photos or helpful clues while Gwen was basking in her own reflection. It occurred to him that she hadn't made a peep or as much as a shuffle for a few minutes and wondered if she were still behind him. He turned and saw her checking herself out in the mirror. He moved to the side so she wouldn't see his reflection chuckling at her. He thought it best not to interrupt.

Rook was just as fascinated with her appearance as she was now. He would watch her all day and be happy doing so. Something about her current state-of-mind, whatever it might be, made her seem innocent and pure of heart. Rook missed feeling like the big brother but this was even better. *I will watch over her until she makes me go away. I was meant to find her,* Rook thought confidently.

While mesmerized by her new reflection, she felt something brush against her calve. It scared the living daylights out of her. She resisted the urge to kick and scream—it was not a completely unfamiliar feeling, just one she was not expecting. She looked down to see a large short-haired orange, tan and cream striped cat leaning its body against her leg—tail in the air, curled at the tip. *Finally! A familiar face.*

"Whinny!" Gwen picked up her furry friend, hugged him, kissed him on the cheek, and squeezed him again. Tucking her right arm under his back she flipped him like a baby in her arms—into his favorite position. He lay with his back feet sticking up, head against her arm looking at his surroundings up-side-down. Gwen suspected this was the part he most enjoyed. She carried him slowly to one of the couches. Whinny curled up in her lap purring like a small moped—Gwen swore he had the loudest purr she'd ever heard.

Rook was elated to see she managed to find someone, or something familiar. "So, you definitely live here. The memories should just come pouring in now," he said hopeful.

Gwen's mood and expression were the opposite of his expectation. She sighed and stroked Whinny's fur. She shook her head and felt like she might start to tear up. "Something isn't right. Actually, nothing is right."

"How so? Maybe I can help you figure it out." He sat next to her and put his hand on her shoulder. "Look, whatever it is, we'll figure it out together. I'm not going to abandon you," Rook said sincerely.

"You will want to abandon me once you realize I'm crazy!"

"Crazy is just an opinion anyway. Consider it a unique characteristic." He smiled in an attempt to lighten the mood but it was not his words nor smile that made her feel better.

Gwen focused on the fact that he had his hand on her, causing the magnet in her center to radiate outward—as if warm water poured from his hand into her shoulder, then throughout her body; soothing. "Why are you so willing to stand by me? You don't know me."

"In my defense, *you* don't really know you either. Am I right?"

Gwen shifted her glance to the floor and continued to stroke Whinny's fur. Rook gave her a moment to process though he was dying to pry for more information.

"How about a tour around the neighborhood?" Rook suggested.

"Sounds good," Gwen agreed, *I need to get out of this house anyway.*

"This neighborhood does look familiar, but different than I remember," Gwen said as she observed the finer details—Rook did nothing to interrupt her focus—it resembles mine, but there aren't as many houses, and they are spaced further apart. "Everyone takes good care of their landscape, that's for sure."

Rook's face twisted into confusion. He wiped the expression as soon as he caught himself making it.

The ground was free of garbage, empty water bottles, and candy wrappers. Her dreamworld was the picture of perfection. The streets were empty and there was no traffic to be heard, no sirens, no dogs barking, no children playing outside. The only audible sound was the birds chirping and the wind blowing through the trees. Not only the sound, but the smell of the trees, grass, and flowers soothing too.

They were just about to the end of the block when suddenly, a large dark orange object shot around the corner, in the street, headed in their direction. Paralyzed by shock; left frozen in time with her jaw hanging open, she stared in awe. The vehicle flew two feet from the ground—silently—zipping past them unbelievably fast. Wide-eyed, she watched it until it was no longer visible, which did not take long. A car, not unlike the one that brought her here—hovered above the street somehow. *I didn't hear the engine and there was no drag as it moved, the way it maneuvered that corner—unreal.* She tried not to act too surprised in Rook's presence—and managed to do so—for the most part.

33

They made it to the corner of the street. *I know there was a submarine sandwich shop on this corner,* Gwen thought, but no sandwich shop existed, just an empty field of grass and wild flowers. *There should be a bank across the street from the sub shop.* This was gone too, replaced by large trees—too large to have been planted recently.

"Something wrong?" Rook was bursting at the seams with questions and saw no harm in letting this one out.

Gwen looked at him as if wrong had been an obvious understatement. "You could say that." Her thoughts raced. "Maybe wrong isn't the right word—different. I remember this intersection differently. Impossibly different," she added to emphasize the point.

Rook realized one day just wasn't going to be enough. "Do you see that brown sign down the street, a block or so down?" He pointed. "I work there—practically live there. If I'm not there, someone will know where to find me." Rook looked more serious now, "If you need anything—anything at all—please don't hesitate to ask me. I can only imagine what you must be going through," he said sympathetically.

Gwen felt her center swirl again. Her cheeks ached as they flushed. "You have no idea how much that means to me."

"I want to take you somewhere. A park not far from here." Rook's beautiful eyes widened, complimented by his smile.

Gwen could hardly contain the excitement she felt within—like goosebumps on the inside of her flesh, "Sounds great. It's not like I have anywhere to be right now," she joked.

34

Chapter Four

The earth-tone brown straw-like stuff had grown close together and stood six feet tall. A narrower dirt path branched out from where they began. Gwen realized she had been so deep in thought that she didn't remember how they got there.

Rook motioned with his hand for her to go ahead of him into the straw labyrinth. She looked at him with a hint of panic. Oddly, Rook felt less like a stranger and more like a lifelong friend. *If I get lost in here, my sense of direction will surely leave me to die,* Gwen thought.

He motioned a second time with raised eyebrows. Gwen made full eye contact. All fear fell away, she suddenly felt like it didn't matter if she were walking into a cave of fire. She felt so safe with him by her side. Her trust was normally not earned so easily.

"You should walk in front of me. I know my way around well and I think it better to keep my eye on you, so you don't get lost," Rook suggested.

She started down the variably curvy path, forked paths came and went along the journey. Rook guided her verbally.

"You come here often?" Gwen asked.

"I do. It's peaceful. It feels like home to me. Home before tragedy stuck."

She heard the faint smile in his voice as he spoke. *I wonder how many people he has taken on this little field-trip.* Gwen wondered if she'd have gone in so willingly if it had been anyone else. *Yea right!*

Rounding another curve Gwen saw light shining in ahead. *Finally, we will be out of this claustrophobic maze.*

Exiting the maze she felt the breeze on her skin again. The surroundings were natural like in the garden behind the house only much larger. Small waterfalls and a stream scattered through the park—nothing like the Michigan parks she was used to. A few large rocks, almost the size of cars, set in the grass. *This is how heaven must look,* she thought. Gwen took in the smell of grass, flowers, and the trees.

Rook broke from a daze and turned his head to look at her. He spoke openly, as if he knew her forever. "So what's your story Penguin?" he asked looking her straight in the eyes.

Gwen turned to face a tree in the distance as she spoke. It was easier to stay focused this way. "Oh, where to start...

"I was raised by my grandparents. My mother gave me up because she was too screwed up to handle motherhood. She was institutionalized shortly after birthing me. Grandma says she was delusional and suicidal. I guess it's a good thing I wasn't under her care. I may have wound up like one of those babies you hear about; murdered by their postpartum-depressed mothers."

Rook's expression changed from calm to confused, concerned, and then back to neutral. He looked as if he wanted to say something but didn't interrupt her story. *He really does want to know more about me,* she thought. *Guys don't pay attention to me, let alone ask for my life story.* Not that she gave them much of a chance. *Maybe I'm more superficial than I thought. Perhaps if I were prettier in my world...* she shook off the thought and regained focus.

Rook smiled at her—obviously having a battle inside her head. Gwen was relieved that he didn't push for more details. She didn't want to scare him away with her personal drama—guys usually tucked tail and ran at the first whiff of drama. The thought of that happening with him bothered her more than she thought it should.

"What's that?" she pointed.

"I call it the sanctuary. It's been in my family for generations. It's just a big empty room really."

Gwen turned to face him as he spoke—rather than at the ground. His eyes felt like a magnetic pulling on her soul—like nothing she had ever experienced before and she didn't know if she could even explain it without sounding corny or cliche; one of those *had to be there* kind of things.

They walked toward a gigantic tree, approximately five feet in diameter. A thick branch grew out the side of the trunk, which curved down and out, then back up. Another branch forked out; fanned out half way on each side—resembling a giant catchers mitt. The branches looked to be hundreds of years old, thicker than any tree Gwen ever saw.

Rook approached the large tree, squatted down and leaped 10 feet up onto the large curved branch. Gwen's jaw dropped! Rook crouched on the limb to look at her. "Well, come on," he said.

"Uh—I don't think so," Gwen said hesitantly.

"What? Is your leg injured?"

"No. It's just that—I'm afraid I'll fall."

"Don't be ridiculous. I won't let you fall. Don't you trust me?"

Gwen bit her lip, pulled her eyebrows together and bounced her knees lightly to warm up. With a deep sigh she shook the nervousness from her hands and wrists. She crouched down the way Rook had, and then sprung up toward the branch. She felt weightless, as if gravity turned a blind eye to her for a brief moment.

Rook stood ready to catch her in case her landing was unstable. She put a little more force into the leap than necessary, clearing the jump too easily. She knocked him backward onto one of the forks in the tree's over-sized catcher mitt. He caught her as she fell on top of him. Rook looked stunned for a moment and then he began to shake with laughter.

Gwen was so embarrassed, but hearing him laugh made her laugh too. She pushed herself up, turned and plopped her butt down on the other forked branches next to him—Rook stayed where he was. *I hope I didn't paralyze him from the fall,* Gwen thought. He put his hands above his head staring out into nature—he looked content and at peace again. Gwen laid back and made herself comfortable. *It feels like this tree was built for this,* she thought. The branches contoured their bodies, lending support in all of the essential areas.

A few quiet minutes passed. Then the laughter crept back up on Gwen. At first, it was more of an internal shaking, which grew louder. Rook started laughing because Gwen was laughing. They laughed so hard, tears came out —followed by laughter without sound. This was the most fun either of them had since... Neither of them let their sorrows ruin the moment.

They were quiet again. Smiling, Rook turned his head to look at Gwen. She could feel the permanent grin etched on her face.

"I've never done that before," she said brushing a tear from under her eye.

"Which part? Jumping in a tree, pushing someone over, or laughing until your ribs split?"

"The first two for sure, and as for the last one—it's been a really long time."

"Glad I was here to see it," Rook chuckled.

"I'm really glad you were here or I wouldn't have had such a comfortable landing."

"Anytime," he replied.

"You asked for it," she reminded him.

"I didn't ask for you to tackle me—that was just a bonus."

Gwen blushed and looked back out to the open park at the perfect weather—not too hot, not too cold, the breeze was light and warm. Gwen didn't know if she could be any more content than she was in this moment. Being *this* close to him made her want to be closer still. The sensation reminded her of when two magnets were near one another—the closer they got, the stronger the attraction. Gwen fantasized about cuddling up in his arms, the way she had been just a few moments ago, and now that the humor and shock of it all were gone, she could really feel that need. It felt more like a need than a want. Not like a physical attraction; but purely spiritual. When their bodies touched, it activated something deep within the center of her being; the core of her soul. To be away from him—even just a few feet—felt like disconnecting from some life force. Ripples of heat throbbed and radiated, from her chest, rippling out to her shoulders, down her arms, and into her fingertips—an intoxicating sensation. *I doubt such feelings are reversible*, she thought. Her feelings felt as permanent as brain damage.

"You said your mother was institutionalized for having delusions?" Rook asked curiously.

Wow, interesting conversation starter, she thought awkwardly. "That's what I've been told."

"In that case, we have more in common than our bird names. A few years ago my father was institutionalized—self-committed. I do think it's for the best. Not because he's delusional but because of the overwhelming guilt he feels. I fear he may try to kill himself. The doctors say that his mind is broken and that his delusions help him cope with what happened. They say that this is the way the mind protects itself from cracking further."

He paused and leaned the back of his head against the branch, staring up into the heart of the tree. "My father was driving my mother and sister to the book house. I'm not sure exactly what happened—I wasn't there. Distracted by something he veered into on-coming traffic, yanked the wheel too hard, spun the car out of control and hit a tree. My mother died shortly after impact, my sister has been in a coma since. The hopes of her coming out of it are slim-to-none. She was only eight years old when this happened. When I visit her she looks so peaceful, like a sleeping angel. My father is considered mentally incompetent so the decision to pull the plug is in my hands," Rook sighed.

"That's awful! How do you keep from losing your mind too? I mean, you pretty much lost your entire family." Gwen's reaction was a human emotional reflex.

He turned his head to look toward her. She could see pain behind his beautiful eyes. *Why is he telling me all of this? Laying out his personal business to a complete stranger. Maybe he feels like he owes me a story in return for the bit I shared with him earlier. Could such a great guy, honestly, not have a better place to be right now?*

Rook continued his intriguing life story, "I keep my mind occupied with work, and school. I also meditate. When I visit this park, I feel at peace. Raven and I came here to play when we were little. We used to improvise telling stories—I would make up part, she would come up with another part. We took turns alternating the story just prior to sunrise."

"Sounds like you were really close." *I can't believe he's telling me this!*

"We were. She looked up to me so much. She knew I would always be there for her. But I couldn't be there for her that day." He closed his eyes as he spoke, visualizing her lying in the hospital—trying not to think about how she looked those first few weeks. He kept his eyes closed a moment longer to keep from falling apart altogether. He had not planned on going into such detail but there was something about Gwen that made him feel safe and carefree. Feelings, which felt familiar; like a shadow cast from a distant memory.

Gwen felt the deepest sympathy for his loss. She too, had lost someone—only a few years back. Baylee had been like a sister. Gwen decided not to tell him this story now. She would not want him to think she was comparing scars. She hated when people did it to her.

She reached her hand out to squeeze his arm wishing desperately to ease his sorrow. The pit of her stomach hurt, watching him suffer—as if the pain were her very own. He was accepting of her touch, and after half a minute, he relaxed. She sensed his mood change like a guitar coming into tune.

"Wow. That's quite an ability you have," he said smiling at her now.

"Ability?" she asked.

"Yeah. What do you call it?" he asked excitedly.

"I don't understand what you mean." Gwen looked just as confused as she felt.

His eyes widened with sudden alert. "You mean, you didn't know you were doing it? Hasn't anyone ever mentioned it? Oh yeah, head injury," Rook reminded himself. It's like you diluted my sorrow and now it's gone.

When you touched me, I felt it break apart and then drift away. Then it was warm, followed by a painless electrical sensation," he recalled.

She removed her hand from his arm. "And now?"

"It feels like some kind of aftershock. It sort of tickles."

"I had no idea." Gwen played the amnesia card in a panic.

"I definitely have a good excuse to see you regularly now," he said astounded by this new revelation. "If only I'd met you sooner," he added.

"Let's not get ahead of ourselves. I'm sure there is a good logical explanation for what happened. Maybe you are just starved for human contact," Gwen suggested.

"Dang! How lonely do you think I am?" Rook knew she was right, but showed his defensive side. He wondered if she read minds too.

She arched an eyebrow and tilted her head. He knew that she saw right through him. "Fine. I'm a loner. I work and I go home, my friends don't bother with me anymore, and I spend my time obsessing over how I'm going to fix Raven. I have the ability to manipulate objects but I don't have the power to repair whatever is going on in her head. Doctors don't even know why she is in a coma."

Gwen—overwhelmed by sight, sound, thoughts, and his presence—felt like a C-student. *He seems comfortable with me. I'm not sure that's a good thing.* His companionship made her feel good, but that was her own selfishness getting the best of her.

"You say you can manipulate objects. Did you mean that literally? Are you an illusionist?"

"I can change objects into other objects of relatively the same size and material properties. It really comes in handy when I'm working. If I need to switch wrench sizes, voile."

"Wow. Really? Change something for me."

"Hmm—let me think." He looked dazed and then his

eyes widened. "Okay. Follow me."

He stood from his lounge and reached his hand out to help her up. He wrapped his arm around her waist and said, "hang on." She knew what he was doing and didn't mind—she was too distracted by him holding her close. They jumped out of the tree onto the ground. Gwen expected it to hurt but they were like cats landing on their feet.

They walked toward the stream, next to another large tree. This one not nearly as big as the last. He bent down and picked up a river rock.

"What is your favorite color?" he asked.

"I like colors in combination."

"Okay. Name your favorite combination."

"Purple and black."

"Works for me," he said smiling confidently.

He put his free hand in hers, squeezed the rock into his other fist, and closed his eyes. He concentrated for a few seconds, then opened his fist to reveal a shiny gold ring. Set in the gold lay a bird-shaped from black onyx, with a gold beak and feet. The eye carved from amethyst.

Gwen gasped, "This is the most beautiful piece of jewelry I ever saw in my life! Not that I've seen much. The craftsmanship is amazing!"

He held it out toward her and said, "Something to remember me by. It should fit if you want to wear it."

She was in complete disbelief. "Impossible," Gwen said in a daze as she placed the ring on her middle finger—it fit perfectly. She stood speechless staring at the impossibly beautiful ring.

Rook backed up and squatted down to sit against the tree. His hands rested locked together on his stomach. Gwen wondered if this took energy out of him or if this were as effortless as skipping a rock across the river. She sat next to him with her back against the tree unable to take her eyes off the ring.

"It was just a rock. How did you turn it into gold and jewels? Are they real?"

"Gold, amethyst, and onyx are all periodic elements either naturally or by some natural occurring process. I was able to derive and alter the rocks natural properties in order to manifest them. Of course they are real." Rook gave her a look as if it were the strangest question he had ever heard.

"So, you could turn rocks to diamonds?"

"Yeah, I suppose I could. Diamonds are so plain though. I prefer stones with color. All in all, they are just rocks."

"And you think my ability is special," Gwen said sarcastically.

"Hey, you want to try something with me?" Gwen asked.
"Definitely!"

"You don't even know what I'm going to suggest." Gwen snickered.

"Let's hear it."

"Well, I was thinking—maybe I could focus on something and see if you can identify the feeling. If it matches mine, then it works. If not then, I guess it was just a coincidence.

"Sounds fun. I have the perfect place."

Chapter Five

As they approached the building Gwen noticed it was built from stone much like her porch. The building looked to be the size of a 400 square-foot shed. The door was made of wood, which looked very old and weathered. Rook put his hand to an oval flat black patch on the door, which reminded her of a small blackboard. A few seconds later there was a latching sound—like a bank vault. The five-inch thick door popped open.

Rook walked in and waved Gwen to follow. She entered the room and heard the massive door close along with the locking sounds behind them. The size from the outside was an optical illusion. The inside looked to be 2,000 square feet. Though there were no windows it wasn't dark inside. The tall ceiling had a large fancy dome skylight. The light—which was dimmer than the light inside the room—funneled down from the skylight into the center of the room where a large stone table stood. The table made from eight-inch thick marble, which matched the floor but the tiles alternated matte to glossy. Four large matte tiles outline by 12 glossy tiles. The edges perpendicular to the walls; making the square tiles appear diamond-shaped.

"My great-grandfather Xanthopsar built this structure with his father when he was 17. He came here to think and pray—it was his personal spiritual sanctuary. When his older brother Curaeus—my great-uncle—became terminally ill their father stopped coming here. Of all times to

45

stop praying I never understood why he would stop then.

When Curaeus died Xanthopsar was forbidden to return to this place because of his father's loss of faith."

"Is there a reason why all of your relatives names revolve around black birds?" Gwen asked.

"I'm sure there is, but I've always just assumed it was a tradition that formed and no one wanted to be the one to break the chain. Our family has been traced back to the 1600s on my father's side. We don't know who started it or why, it's just always been that way."

"Wouldn't you run out of names eventually?" Gwen knew the answer as soon as she heard herself ask.

"There are juniors and thirds and repeats of earlier generation names. I share the same name as an ancestor from the 1800s."

"Have you thought about what you will name your children?"

"I am considering Jay, if a son. I am undecided on a daughter's name."

"Aren't Jays blue?"

"Blue Jays are blue. There are Jays which are black," Rook replied.

"Jay is a good name. More common—no offense."

"None taken."

"I have another question for you," Gwen said, fascinated by the topic.

"Go for it."

"If your great grandfather Xan... uh..."

"Xanthopsar," he corrected.

"Yeah, him. If he was forbidden to come here, how are you able to?"

"Well, it's not like he put a curse on the place or anything. There is nothing to keep me out. Not even the locks."

"So that sound was a locking mechanism," Gwen

confirmed.

"The internal bolting system is like a vault. It's partly the reason why the door is so thick, and heavy too."

"So, you're not supposed to be in here?"

"My father was always curious about this place but never knew how to get in. He told me stories as a child, which fascinated me. I came to this park to play, and then later on with Raven. We would make-believe that it was a magical fortress. One day when I was out by myself—I was pretending again—I placed my hand on the black plate and imagined the door opening. I imagined it so clearly—as if I knew it would open—then it did. It scared the heck out of me. At first I didn't realize that I actually opened the door. I thought someone was inside, coming out. I ran home and didn't return for a few days. I didn't try to open the door again for about a month. I needed time to mentally prepare myself for what I might find inside. I reran the old stories through my head until I convinced myself there was nothing to be afraid of.

"Did you ever bring your father here?" Gwen asked intrigued.

"I couldn't bring myself to tell him I had opened the door. He had all of these fantasies built up in his head of what it would be like, and what was inside. I couldn't ruin it for him. I think he would be disappointed to learn there was nothing here—no magic, nothing from the past left lingering behind. And because I didn't tell him, I couldn't tell Raven either. She would most likely give in and ruin the secret, thus ruining the magic this place held for our father."

"So, what is it you do here?"

"I sit or lay on that platform, let the light from above shine down on me and imagine I'm being brought back from the dead. I can't think of another way to describe the contrasting difference I feel within myself afterward. I feel like I can breathe better, see better, and think more clearly. All of my senses are refreshed and I feel more in tune with the earth, plants, and animals.

"Sounds nice. Do you think you could show me?"

"I'm hoping it will be amplified during the experiment. I've never tried anything like this before—never with someone. I guess we can kill two birds with one stone. Ha-ha, get it?"

Gwen looked at him and didn't even need to comment.

"Hey, I couldn't refuse," Rook defended his lame joke.

"That's fine and all, but please, let's leave out the killing part. We're the only two birds I see in here. You're a nice guy and all, but the whole double suicide thing—not for me," Gwen joked.

She was flattered that she was the only one he attempted this with. *We hardly know each other and he is already doing things with me that he has never done with anyone else.* A song began to play in Gwen's head: *Like a Virgin* by *Madonna.* The meaning was significant in so many ways. Everything in this world, though somewhat similar was still a completely new experience for her. It irritated her how the song just pried it's way into her head while she was trying to focus on Rook.

They sat cross-legged, facing one another on the marble table. Gwen could see why he found the place relaxing. The room had an old castle appeal without the dust. The room was so clean she wondered if Rook was a neat-freak.

"Okay, now what?" she asked.

"I'll rest my hands palm-down on my knees. You rest

your hands palm-down on mine. Close your eyes, breathe in through your nose, and out through your mouth. Breathe from deep within your chest, not from the top. Count down from 10 slowly. By the end of the countdown you should feel relaxed. Once you have relaxed, pick an emotion and try projecting it to me. I'll let you know if I feel any different."

Rook was excited about sharing the experience with her. He liked the trust Gwen showed him. It fulfilled the protector in him. He had not realized how much he hungered for that energy until now.

Gwen was skeptical about the whole experience. *Even if it turns out I have no special gift, the moment will still be worth it.* She shook out her wrists and sighed. *Here we go.* She placed her hands on his, as suggested, then closed her eyes. She began to count down from 10 slowly with each deep breath, as Rook suggested.

10—she felt a wave of warmth come in through her head and out of her chest. Nine—it felt like she was spinning. Eight—spinning faster. Seven—she no longer felt the spinning. Six—her pulse beat louder in her ears. Five— she could no longer physically feel her body or her breathing. Four—ripples of gentle dizziness vibrated from her head downward into her body, and then out through her limbs. Three—the vibrations intensified. Two—it felt like something heavy pushed against her body. One—the vibrations—combined with the heaviness—collided and there was a silent explosion. The blast made her gasp and suddenly her eyes were open. She was no longer in a sitting posture in the sanctuary.

This reminded her of the way her body felt before— like she had driven over rumble strips—and the strange, unfamiliar territory. *Did I fall asleep during the experiment? I felt conscious the whole time.*

Gwen's surroundings were a dark gray haze. The

breeze was cool and constant, there wasn't a tree in sight, the ground felt solid though it appeared to be nothing more than sand, and rocks.

Gwen heard Rook's voice calling her in the distance. Unable to tell what direction it came from—as if coming from all directions, echoing in the emptiness. She tried to call back but no sound came from her throat. She heard herself in her thoughts but could not physically speak. Even if she could, there were no landmarks in sight to describe. How would he find her?

Panic flowed through her and suddenly it was like someone shut the lights out on her. Her body snapped sharply. Gwen's eyes popped open as her body jolted forward with intense force. Her vision hazy but she could see she was back on the marble table. Rook's eyes were open too, filled with panic.

"Whoa! What was that? Are you alright?"

Gwen shook her head to clear the daze. Her wide eyes met his, "I don't know. It was like I was dreaming."

Rook was amazed and in shock as he spun himself around on the platform. His legs dangled over the edge. "I think that's enough experimentation. What do you say?" Rook pieced the events together in his mind and began to wonder about Gwen's true abilities.

Gwen nodded and waited for him to say more. Scooting herself to sit next to him on the platform. Her legs dangling next to his.

"I guess this wasn't what you had in mind?" Gwen snickered. "What about you? Did you see anything?"

"Yeah. The back of my eyelids," he said chuckling.

"I heard you calling to me but I couldn't speak," she explained.

"You heard me? You looked unconscious except your eyelids were fluttering like hummingbird wings. I was afraid you were having a seizure or something."

"Your eyes were supposed to be closed!" Gwen said horrified. She didn't want to imagine what it must have looked like from his perspective. The thought made her feel awkward and insecure.

Rook continued, "I was anxious all of a sudden and I was afraid to keep my eyes closed," he explained. "Like something or someone was behind me. That's when I tried to bring you out of it. When you didn't respond I panicked even more."

"Maybe I do have this weird gift you're talking about. If that's what it is, I don't know how I'm supposed to control it."

"What were you so scared of? It must have been terrifying!"

"Like I said, it was like a bad dream. Not bad, but eerie."

Gwen explained the best her recollection would allow. Rook was so engrossed in her story, Gwen was tempted to make something up just to keep his intent stare on her.

"That's it? I thought you were being chased by someone or something."

"Some of the fear you felt, may have been your own. You could have been afraid of feeling afraid," Gwen said.

"How about next time you try and focus on something more positive," Rook countered.

"Next time? Pwuh—forget it."

Rook turned his head up to face the dome skylight, "We should get going."

"Already?" her voice asked disappointed. She didn't want the day to be over so soon. Her heart sunk into the pit of her stomach. Her legs kicked as they dangled over the edge of the marble table top. "Come over. We can try again if you want. Or we could just hang out," she suggested.

"Not tired of me yet?" Rook joked with his sideways

glance.

"Nope," she smiled.

Rook smiled and she could feel her soul turning itself inside-out again. *How does he do that?* she wondered, irritated by her idiocy. She had the overwhelming urge to wrap her arms around him and hold him close to her for as long as possible. *Ridiculous!* she thought. That thought intensified the pulling sensation and she became lightheaded. Gwen stumbled sideways removing herself from the platform. Rook grabbed her arm to keep her from falling.

"You aright? After effect from the exercise?" Rook assumed.

"Must be," she lied.

They walked back through the park silently. Gwen guessed Rook was as deep in thought as she was. She was right. Rook had never experienced anything quite like it himself. The experience reaffirmed his earlier suspicions that this girl was special. This experience intensified his intrigue.

Gwen thought about the dark place. The way the gray clouds swirled through the sky, sand blew across the ground beating against the calf of her jeans, Rook's voice calling from all directions. *No sense in trying to rationalize anything. Normal in my world and normal in this world are obviously not even close to being the same.*

The sky was changing in a way she wasn't used to. The darkness crept up from the horizon, slowly gaining on them from the East. The daylight faded from the ground first. The sun cast a shadow on Rook's world which consumed the daylight as it rose.

Gwen didn't want Rook to go. The magnet in her center radiated outward again. She held her hand out and said, "Thank you so much for the ring."

Rook reached for Gwen's fingertips, turned her hand down angling in the last light of day. He smiled with distant eyes as he let go of her hand Gwen's fingers curled in an attempt to keep his hand from leaving hers. It was an unconscious, subtle reflex. Either he didn't notice or he didn't mind. Gwen didn't care either way.

Rook used the ride home to think. His mind had been running on auto-pilot for the last few days. His life had changed in the blink of an eye. All because he forgot his guitar. *It's amazing how something so insignificant can bring about such a large change—ripples.* He knew that ripples had the potential to form into great tidal waves over time. He wanted to remain optimistic about his time with Gwen, but there was a small twinge in his gut that begged for attention. Rook knew he couldn't ignore it forever, but for now, all he wanted was to enjoy the happiness for however long it lasted. *I will not get my hopes up,* he thought. No matter how much he reassured himself the twinge was not satisfied. He felt like yelling at himself, "What the heck is your problem? What do you want?"

Was it guilt? It wasn't wrong to move on with his life and he knew that. His family would have wanted it for him. His mother would be so excited that Rook met a girl, especially such a genuine sweetheart as Gwen. Knowing his mother would never meet his future wife, and children, made his eyes wet. Rook knew his mother was not lost forever, but it saddened him that he could have no communication with her, or see the expressions on her face anymore. He missed hearing her laugh. He missed them all as a family unit.

Maybe I just feel guilty because I put Raven off to see Gwen the night I saved her. Rook knew that hadn't been it, but he was trying to reason with himself.

The dark began to rise quickly. As the sun crept up behind the trees, darkness swallowed everything in its angle of projection. Rook made it into the house just in time to shut the shades. He planned to stay up late to redirect his thinking on the more positive highlights of the day. He would not go to bed feeling sorry for himself.

He thought about Gwen's quirkiness, which calmed him faster than he expected. Usually, sitting in the large empty house was depressing but tonight his mind was preoccupied. Thinking about Gwen made him worry for her. *It must be strange only remembering fragments about life.* Rook was no medical major, but he found her sort of amnesia to be rather odd. He didn't think she was faking, and he was pretty sure she wasn't crazy. *I can live with crazy,* Rook chuckled alone.

Rook wanted to show Gwen the world as he knew it. There just wasn't enough time in a day. The next semester of college was approaching. He felt a slight sinking feeling in the pit of his stomach. That meant they would spend less time together. *Ah, she could be sick of me by then, or remember her friends and family; forgetting all about me and my little adventures. Once her memory fully resurfaces she may realize I'm not all that much fun to be around—once all the mystery is gone.* Rook hit the palm of his hand against his forehead. *Don't go there Rook! Big dummy! Focus on the now.* Rook fully believed in living in the moment but he found himself micro-managing these moments and didn't like it.

Chapter Six

Gwen plopped down on the couch with her legs stretched out. A million images racing through her mind, at the speed of light. Whinny let out a short meow. Gwen looked toward the edge of the couch and saw his face looking back at her. "Hey Whinny. Come on." She patted the couch cushion. He hopped up and laid down alongside of her. There was a familiar jingling noise as he lay. Curiously, Gwen reached for his name tags.

"Chester," Gwen read aloud. "Chester? Really?" she asked aloud. She flipped the tag over to see another name and address. Alexa Larissa Murdock followed by the house address. "Oh, sounds mysterious. Pleasure to meet you, I am Alexa Murdock but you can call me Lex." Gwen chuckled at herself.

Chester purred and smiled his squinted eye cat grin. Gwen thought this must have been Chester and Alexa's routine every night; no different from when Whinny and she lie in bed together. He smiled and purred at her just the same. Chester didn't seem to know the difference, or he just didn't care.

I asked Rook to come in and hang out with me for a bit but he refused. Maybe he senses that I am crazy about him and he was trying to let me down easy. Illogical, we made plans to see each other all week. Gwen wished with all of her heart she could call Baylee and tell her about this amazing journey and about the awesome guy she met.

Gwen lay stroking Chester's soft fur as she

daydreamed. *I wonder what would happen if I did the count-down alone. Would anything strange happen without Rook's presence?*

She began the count-down from where she lay. This time the spinning sensation was not as intense. This was more of a gentle rocking sensation—like a hammock rocking in the breeze. This imagery intensify the swaying feeling followed by a low buzzing sound in her head. *I don't remember hearing that before.* She felt the heaviness on her body again. *I know I'm close now.* She waited patiently— staying calm was key. Focusing on the heaviness she tried to intensify the sensation. The fluttering in her chest began. *I forgot about this part.* The countdown was complete, and now she focused on her breathing and nothingness. Faint shades of black swirled behind her eyelids. Some of the black shades took on a blue tint others green. Watching the colors swirl reminded her of watching a large globe spin. The blue-black, like the water and the green-black, like the continents. The forms swirled around each other luring her into unconsciousness.

The images formed into trees, and grass, swaying in the breeze before being abruptly sucked away from her in blackness, leaving her shivering in the cold sandy dark place. Sand blasted her right cheek—far worse than her first encounter in this place. She heard something in the wind—a low growl with periodic snapping sounds. It reminded her of a stiff plastic bag whipping in a tree.

She began walking though she had no sense of direction. Resisting the urge to stand there dumbfounded she progressed toward a small hill in the distance. As she got closer to the hill, sharp black triangles came into focus from behind the hill. Her gut-instinct told her not to go any further. She stood motionless for a moment as the wind growled even louder. Suddenly the triangles grew quickly into ears of an orange-eyed, long matted black-haired beast, which was leaping toward her. She turned to run as fast as possible, which felt like slow motion. Gwen knew she could not outrun the beast but tried anyway. She awaited the pain of its inevitable pounce on her back. Everything went black and Gwen felt like she was falling. Falling for what seemed like forever before she could see color again. Her surroundings became green blurs and then she landed on her back.

A tree caught her fall—the catchers' mitt tree from the park. Gwen was no longer in Alexa-form. She was her bland, ordinary self; not attractive enough for this world. Realizing that she was not in a body compatible with this world also meant she was stuck in the tree. Bev's voice called from a distance. She stood waving to Gwen near the straw brush. Gwen wanted nothing more than to run to her grandmother. She tried to call to her grandmother but her voice was weak and thin.

Three of the orange-eyed beasts prowled from behind her grandmother. Gwen tried to yell louder, "Run! Grandma run!" No use—the words came out paper thin again. Acid churned through her body. She leaped from the tree and was suddenly was running faster than humanly possible—even for this world. All of her fear was gone in that instant as she rushed to save her grandmother from the beasts. Her eyes locked on the beast to her left. The beast leaped six feet in the air toward her. She took a flying leap toward the beast. Their bodies collided and tumbled to the ground. Rolling around she heard a growl come from within her own chest. Her hands were like those of a large jungle cat, her claws enormous and sharp as she ripped through the beast's flesh like butter. She felt the warmth of it against her paws as she mangled it. The smell of its blood sweet like cherries, bitter-sweet like ginger. She had no desire to taste it, only breathe its fresh sweet aroma. As the creature lay lifeless, the smell faded.

She turned to see the other beasts backing away slowly, growling—their eyes stayed locked on hers. The battle was over, but there was a part of her that wanted to fight them anyway. If not for the fun of it, then for the smell alone.

Gwen turned to look at Bev but she was gone. She called for her in the brush, but no sound came out. The beasts were gone too. Gwen hoped they had not gone looking for her grandmother. She looked at her hands and found they were human again, still covered in blood but the smell no longer appealed to her.

Suddenly, everything began to spin around her slowly, and her feet were heavy. She tried to pull her knee up to free a foot from the ground, but it was stuck. Both feet were stuck. She felt herself shrinking and then realized she was not shrinking; but sinking into the ground. Her knees were now underground and felt like stone—immobile. Her heart pounded in her ears. As her heart beat faster, she sunk into the ground faster. Her surroundings were still spinning as if she were a pivot pin stuck into the ground. As parts of her body sank into the ground, they submerged in quick-setting concrete. Fearing what would happen to her torso as it became submerged—lungs no longer able to expand—sweat began to bead on her forehead and she could hear her heart beating in her ears, louder than ever.

Suddenly, the sky turned into black swirling clouds. Thunder and lightning crashed above. It looked as though a tornado was forming directly overhead. The lightning flashed across the sky in constant unrelenting intervals. The swirling clouds spun in one direction, her surroundings in another. Slowly sinking into her stone-like grave, she felt her chest caving in. Taking in the largest gasp her lungs would allow she hoped this last breath would somehow buy her enough time to escape. As she drew—what was to be—her last breath, she opened her eyes to find that she was still on the couch.

That was the worst nightmare I've ever had in my life! These bodies must have more intense dreams too!

Gwen looked down and saw Chester curled up next to her. Little cat snores escaped his partially opened mouth. One foot gave a quick jerk every now and again. He looked so precious that Gwen felt the warmth ripple through her chest and throb down her arms. *Everything I feel is like one hundred times that of my normal feelings. It's like this body is more sensitive to emotion or it has a larger emotional threshold. I must have been out for a long time. The windows are already starting to darken.* They were not just dimming; darkness swallowed part of the surrounding living room. Darkness poured in the way sunlight did in her world.

Exhausted, she decided to sleep in Alexa's bed rather than the couch. She took her time preparing for bed. Hoping enough time would pass to shake off the bad dream so it was less likely to return.

The skylight dome above the bed stopped her in her tracks. Funneling down nothing but blackness the way it would have funneled sunshine during the day. Darkness engulfed the entire bed. She approached the darkness and reached a finger out to touch it, as if it were an inanimate object. Her finger disappeared into the darkness. She reached her hand in further and watched it disappear. Fearfully, she quickly yanked her hand back. She reached into the darkness once more; this time in an effort to find the bed. The cozy comforter was there beneath her grip. As Gwen pondered climbing into the blackness to sleep, she was surprised to see Chester from her periphery. He leaped into the darkness without fear. She heard his claws fluffing the blankets. *Well, if it's good enough for him, it's good enough for me.*

Lying in the bed looking to the darkness, she analyzed memories of the things Rook said as well as his body language—molding their meanings to suit her personal preference. She thought about lying in their tree together, but in her version she doesn't get up to sit next to him— she lay with him holding her close. The depressing conversation about their losses replaced by laughter. As they lie there enjoying the faint breeze blowing through the trees and their hair, they remain content for hours.

Gwen thought her fantasies would probably seem lame to others, but they were her own. She did not lust for him in the physical sense; the way she probably would if she were in her world. She craved the energy and closeness. *When he is around me, it's like putting a magnet close to a television screen. The television screen is my brain, distorted and warped. My sentences are clumsy, my mental processes are slower and I completely lose concept of time.* This is the conversation she imagined having with her dear old friend Baylee.

As Gwen lie waiting for sleep to grab hold of her, she thought about her grandparents. *Do they realize I am not my usual self? Is Alexa living in my shoes while I live in hers. I wonder if she knows or understands what happened. If she doesn't inhabit my body in the meantime, does my body lay unconscious? What if everyone thought I was dead and they buried me? What if I go back to my embalmed body underground? What if they cremated me?* Her heart quickened, throat tightened as she put herself into a state of panic, not unlike the nightmare she just experienced.

If dark is the absence of light, how the heck can dark be cast over top of light? Of all of the strange happenings she encountered so far, this one really nagged at her.

Tomorrow I figure this out. I can't lay around waiting for answers to come to me. I need to figure this thing out. If I'm insane, fine, I need to know.

Chapter Seven

A sudden loud noise startled Gwen out of her skin. "Oh No!" she gasped.

"Al! I know you're in there!" an unfamiliar female voice yelled from behind the front door. Gwen panicked and quickly made a decision. Just as Gwen began to open the door, she felt it open faster than she pulled it. A young girl —probably 17 years old—barged in with her mouth yapping several miles per minute. Gwen couldn't understand a word of it, but could tell it was important.

Gwen put her hands on the petite girl's shoulders to calm her. "Slow down, I can't understand you! You need to calm down so I can understand what you're saying," Gwen said in a firm, slow pace.

The girl stomped past and plopped down on one of the couches. Gwen stood there blinking in awe. *Strange girl,* she thought.

Gwen sat on the couch across from the girl. "So, what seems to be the problem?" Gwen asked.

The girl leaned forward staring at Gwen as if she were looking for something. Feeling insecure Gwen asked, "What? Do I have something on my face?" Gwen brushed her hand against her cheeks.

"Did you... you know... did you do it?" the girl asked, just above a whisper.

"Did I do what?"

"Oh my gosh! You did!" The girl's eyes widened with excitement.

"You don't know who I am do you?" The girl didn't wait for an answer. "You don't know who you are. I was there, as instructed but you were not. I panicked, but then assumed you chickened-out. How did you get home? When did you get home?"

Gwen interrupted her questioning before she could kick her mouth back into high gear—beyond audible. "I woke up in the hospital. Some guy saw me collapse and took me there."

"Did you have a head scan?" the girl asked panicking. "What hospital did you go to?"

"I uh... I'm not sure. They said it didn't look like much, thought it might be short-term amnesia or something."

The girl blew out an exaggerated sigh. "Short-term amnesia... good." The girl wasn't looking at Gwen anymore —she was buried in thought.

"So. You know what actually happened to me?" Gwen asked.

The girl's face changed into helplessness. "Not exactly, Alexa is the expert on the subject."

"What subject?"

"Wardlows, and the whole epidemic theory," the girl replied. It didn't sound like a good thing. Gwen's instincts told her Alexa was a heroine—maybe even a martyr—and that made her nervous. "What did she get me into?" Gwen asked in a sudden panic. "What is a wardlow?"

Cat put her fist to her chest as if to grab hold of an invisible medallion, closed her eyes and then said, "Cat."

Gwen looked confused and answered, "Yes, the cat is fine. Cats are wardlows?"

Cat's eyes opened wide and then she laughed hysterically. "No! My name is Tabitha, but everyone calls me Cat. You know? Tabby Cat? You... well, Alexa started it. "What do your people call you?"

Gwen cleared her throat as she choked on the question

of her people. "Gwen," she said offering her hand. Cat looked at Gwen's hand unsure what she was doing. Catching on to Cat's confusion she attempted to replicate the gestures Cat made prior.

"Nice to meet you, Gwen. We have a lot to talk about."

Gwen was irritated that Cat continued to ignore her question. *Oh well, I probably don't want to know anyway.* But Gwen did want to know, and if Cat wouldn't tell her, she would research it after she left.

Cat led the way to a room full of artwork. In Gwen's world, this was Bev's craft room. Cat stopped in front of a large painting, approximately 4' x 5'. Gwen thought she could stare at the many fine details in the painting for weeks, and still find something new. Though the images were drawn into and out from one another, they were shaded and blended in just the right places to make a smooth transition. Dark red tones, streaks of brown and black blended and whirled together—dark but alluring. Gwen felt somehow connected to the painting from inside —like there was a rope tied to her internal organs—the painting tugged at her. She felt no pain, just pressure and a mixture of emotions she never experienced before.

"Oh my Gosh! It's amazing!" Cat said sympathetically. "I can really feel this work on a deep level." Her glance went off in the distance as she continued, "The love, loss, triumph, mystery and the rest is open to interpretation. I think there is a little something for everyone in this one. Her message will reach a lot of people. I think this one just may have the awakening effect she was hoping for. You know how it goes, those who are ready will be affected," she rolled her eyes while she said it. Cat had very little patience with those who were slow to keep up, and this was obvious to Gwen.

"So, do you understand the clues Alexa left for you?" Cat asked excitedly.

Gwen felt the panic flowing through her again. "Clues?"

The girl sighed hard, "Clues to what Alexa wants you to do next? I'm guessing she painted these pictures for a reason. Oh, she never tells us anything!" Cat was clearly agitated with her best friend right now.

"She didn't exactly leave me an instruction manual. Let me see. I haven't had a chance to..." Gwen picked up a stack of sketches. One of the sketches resembled the garden she had been standing in, there were two figures drawn as shadow—one taller than the other—positioned toward each other. The flowers and trees where sketched in much more detail than the shadowy figures. *Perhaps these were designs she intended to make into paintings later.* Another sketch showed a large close-up of a cat's face— probably inspired by Chester. One of the eyes was a typical cat's eye, the other had no eye in its socket. In place of the eyeball were smaller scaled images. Though Gwen didn't have to squint to see the images, she pulled the paper closer to her face to see if her eyes were deceiving her. Inside the cat's eye was the face of a person —the detailed face of Beverly Penn. *Grandma? Impossible!* The entire experience was impossible. Gwen despised unanswered questions! She knew that most, if not all, of her experiences in this world would never be explained to her.

"This picture! This picture of Whinny shows a reflection of one of my people in his eye."

Cat looked closely at the picture. "This picture just represents your ability to see through animals eyes."

"Really! Alexa could see my grandmother through Whinny's eyes!" Gwen's sense of hopelessness fell out of her like a boulder, and suddenly her spirits were lifted.

"His name is Chester, just so you know," Cat corrected.

"Oh yeah. In my world his name is Whinny," Gwen said. *Could we really have the same kind of cat? The exact same cat?*

Cat was lost in thought again and Gwen wished she could read her mind. She wondered how much Cat was keeping to herself. *A lot,* she guessed. Cat seemed nice enough but Gwen couldn't help but wonder if she could be trusted. Her gut told her that Cat was trustworthy. That would have to do for now.

"The big picture, this new one," Cat pointed at the large picture referred to as Awakening, "this is the one I would be studying if I were you."

"I don't know what I'm looking for! I need to know what happened. How do I get back home? Why am I here? How am I here?" Gwen could go on for hours questioning.

"It's a long story and I think it's best if we had a meeting with the whole group. All I can tell you for sure is: watch your back, and use your intuition—it's pretty good and should still be in tact." Cat looked more serious than any other moment during her visit.

"I have been hanging around Rook, the guy who found me," Gwen explained.

"No! You shouldn't be hanging out with anyone outside of the circle." Cat's eyes widened.

"What? Why? I feel safe when I'm with him," Gwen defended.

"He can't know anything about you. He can't suspect you're different. If anyone finds out about what has gone on and you get caught, we are all going down!"

"I have been doing a good job blending in so far, but there are a few things I don't understand."

"Such as?" Cat asked.

"Why is it dark when the sun rises? Why haven't I been hungry or thirsty since waking? I think this is a good place to start?" Gwen ranted.

Cat looked mesmerized by Gwen's questions. "Wow. This is really happening isn't it?"

Gwen shook her head and gestured for Cat to answer the questions.

"We can't see when the sun rises because we are nocturnal—we sleep when the sun is out. The sun fuels our bodies at night, which is why there is a large dome over the bed. I bet that was weird for you the first time," Cat chuckled.

Gwen laughed, "Yeah I just tried it out for the first time last night."

Cat's face was serious again, "You must sleep in the sunlight. You need the nourishment. That is why Alexa ignited the change outdoors. To give her body a supercharge during the switch," Cat said seriously.

"I slept on the couch the first night I got here. I had nightmares last night so I slept in Alexa's bed. Gwen's tone changed, "We don't eat or drink for nourishment?"

Cat looked confused about the question and answered, "Nourishment is provided by the sun's rays alone. It's natural for us to sleep in the sun, that's why we are naturally blinded by the sun," Cat answered, as if it were obvious.

"Are all animals blinded by the sun?" Gwen asked astonished.

"Not all of them, but they too require nourishment from the sun," Cat added. Cat felt like she was talking to a young child with such basic questions.

"My special ability? I can see through the eyes of animals?" Gwen asked curiously.

"Yes. You can tap into their parietal and occipital receptors; syncing them with your own. Your intuition has gotten better over the years with practice. I don't know if you have any abilities now that you are—well—you. I'm not really sure how that works."

"I don't think I can keep myself away from Rook. I feel drawn to him," Gwen explained.

66

"Oh man! Don't go falling in love while Alexa is away. Or better yet, please do. Alexa needs to get her head out of the books and into life once in a while. She is so driven to fight for these wardlows—I really don't understand the obsession. I don't know why she cares anyway." Cat drifted away in her thoughts again.

"Hang out with your guy friend, learn from him, try to blend in, until I can pull the group together and better train you. Someone is bound to come looking for you soon. Perhaps it's best that you don't stay home for now. But do not, and I repeat, do not let him suspect that you are different from us!" Cat's eyes were serious and they bore holes through her now. "I promise," Gwen nodded.

The thought of her setting Alexa up with Rook made her feel a bit jealous. *Well, what did you think was going to happen? Duh!* Gwen thought. This realization hit deep in the pit of her stomach. She hadn't thought it through—not really. She had been avoiding this—thinking about the consequences of her actions. *It's not fair! I didn't choose this, whatever this is!* Gwen justified to herself. She was so preoccupied with *these* thoughts that Cat's warning about someone coming to look for her, didn't sink in. By the look of concern on her best friend's face, Cat thought that it had.

"Your phone should be in the nightstand," Cat said.

"You have phones here? Sweet!"

Cat gave Gwen another concerned look before backing up to sit in the adjacent sofa chair. Gwen could tell Cat was trying not to stare at her. "It's so weird," Cat began. Gwen waited for her to continue. "You're like a totally different person."

"Helll-ohh?" Gwen defended.

"Yeah but your personality isn't even the same. The way you move is different. The way you speak is different. It's totally obvious."

"Don't worry prematurely. I feel fine. Just a little confused at the moment. You will help me through this, I have full faith in you," Gwen said. She figured feeding her ego might be the best approach.

"But you don't even know me anymore," Cat said dully.

"But I feel like I've known you my entire life," Gwen assured her.

"Alexa has," Cat said sounding as if her friend was gone forever.

"Well, I trust you. Everything is going to be fine," Gwen said.

"Just do me a favor, the phone lines aren't clean, they are always monitored for suspicious activity, so don't use them unless you have to."

Gwen wanted to ask who Cat thought she was going to call but didn't. Cat gave Gwen one last look before leaving, "Maybe Alexa has been right all along—wardlows don't seem like such bad people."

Gwen's curiosity led her to the basement.

Wow! Alexa is so organized. This must be her home office. She walked over to the large desk, which looked ordinary in every way. Even the computer appeared ordinary—she expected something space-aged and high-tech.

Gwen took a seat behind the desk and began pulling at the drawer handles underneath. Some opened and some didn't. It was the drawers that didn't open, which intrigued her most. *Must be something special in these. Where would I put a key? If not a huge secret, I would probably leave it in another drawer.* She pulled open the middle drawer, directly under the desktop, the shallowest drawer of them all. She found a few small keys in the drawer and tried them all. One of the keys opened a semi-secret drawer—containing 50 or more files. Gwen selected a file at random—none of them were labeled. *They are just sketches. Why lock them up? Is she afraid someone will steal them? They're good but not that good. These aren't any ordinary sketches. She is hiding them for a reason. Yet she did not go to extreme lengths to hide them.* Gwen thumbed through a few more and stumbled upon a sketch, which made chills climb her spine. The desolate desert of swirling black clouds. *Has she been here too? Does this place really exist?*

Gwen shoved the sketches back in the file and grabbed another file at random. This file contained pages of typed paragraphs. Though Gwen was curious, she hesitated because of the massive word count she saw on just one of the pages. Thumbing through the pages she saw hand-drawn diagrams. Flipping back to the first page she skimmed the words:

He was attacked by a patient who lost his mind during a voluntary procedure. The patient was injected with the serum to produce the side-effects mimicking that of the wardlow mind-frame.

His death was a tragic accident and an underestimation of the patient's strength. He kept the details of his research from everyone and led them all to believe that he thought the wardlow was simply a person suffering with a rare mental disorder, which could be cured with the right treatment. It wasn't a complete lie, just a non-updated suspicion. The final belief was so far-fetched that he couldn't bring his colleagues into it. He was afraid they would turn him in.

Gwen put the paperwork back into the file and grabbed another. The symbols and diagrams were well beyond that of her high school education. Gwen was into art and literature. She steered clear of the science stuff. Just looking at it overwhelmed her. That's enough for now—it's break-time.

Chapter Eight

Walking around the block Gwen wondered about home. *What if Alexa is rude to Mimic while I'm away? He is probably my only chance at a real relationship once all this fairytale stuff is over with.* Feelings of guilt followed the thought. *I'm getting way ahead of myself. I have to stay in the moment or I'm going to lose my mind for sure!*

Suddenly a burst of energy pulsed through her body. The closer she got to Alexa's house, the more the feeling intensified—resembling an itch she couldn't scratch. Whatever her body wanted, it wanted it now! She took off into a light jog, which brought a small sense of relief. Picking up the pace felt better yet so she kicked into high gear. She circled the block once and then expanded the perimeter to include surrounding blocks until the fourth lap.

Rounding the corner, about to pass the house again, she saw someone standing at her front door. A tall man in a khaki trench coat and matching khaki hat. *Why the jacket? It isn't cold outside; a constant 72 Fahrenheit night or day.* From behind, he reminded her of the lead character from the cartoon *Inspector Gadget*.

Gwen stopped in her tracks to hide behind a bush— unsure why she was hiding. *The man is at the house, he probably knows Alexa,* Gwen wondered. Gwen's grandmother always said, "No matter what, no matter how silly it seems, no matter how illogical, always listen to your instincts, always!" *If I have a gift, it's telling me I don't want him to find me.* From her hiding place, the man appeared to be at least six-foot-three-inches, slender build, blond hair, and most likely silver eyes. His shoes matched his coat and hat. It felt like forever. *I wish he would hurry up and leave already!*

Finally, he turned around, shot a glance around the yard. Then he stepped off the porch and walked down the driveway, and out to the street. His car parked at an angle not visible from where Gwen crouched. She waited a few minutes just to be certain he didn't double back. Her desire to run faded. The man didn't look sinister but there was something off about him. *Cat said to use my intuition.* She began walking slowly—too shaken to go inside the house.

Gwen felt pressure on her right shoulder and a sudden break in silence. Instantly, her body turned ice cold like an arctic blast from within her core, exploding outward. Her body spun counter-clockwise—quick like a cobra. Her body met the resistance of a solid mass encased in something soft and warm. The wind from her sudden lightning-fast movement whizzed past her ears. Once her eyes caught up to her actions, she was stunned and overwhelmed with feelings of guilt. Everything happened so fast and without thought, it caught her by surprise. Not only surprised by what happened but she was surprised to see him. Gwen had not expected to see his face today. Laying on the ground before her, with his wrist, hand and arm twisted in an unnatural manner—was her only true friend in this world. She dropped his hand as fast as she could—as slow as a turtle in comparison to seconds prior.

"Rook! Oh my gosh! I am so sorry! Are you alright?"

Gwen had been so nervous from hiding in the bushes, and deep in thought that she didn't hear him approach.

"I'm okay—just a little dazed. That was not the reaction I was expecting. Holy cow! You're fast—and strong too!

How did you do that?"

Slightly winded from the encounter, she tried to piece the answer together in her head before spitting the words out, but there was no time to edit. She owed him an apology and an explanation fast.

"You scared the living heck out of me! When you put your hand on my shoulder and began talking out of nowhere... it must have triggered some sort of... crazy reflex."

"Luckily, I've had some training and knew how to fall out of that crazy martial move," Rook said thankful. "I took some Hapkido a few years back. I guess you never really forget. I'm just glad I learned how to break-fall before giving up the class! I'd be permanently broken otherwise. I've never had to react so quickly." His shocked expression looked permanent.

"Hap-what-y?" Gwen asked confused.

"Do *not* tell me you have never taken classes!"

I can't explain this one off. Time to think fast. I don't want to lie.

"I—took some kind of martial art when I was little. I can't remember what it was called. I guess it's like you said, the body never forgets."

Rook brushed himself off and began to stand up, shaking his arm out. He was quiet for a minute, which seemed longer because Gwen was desperately waiting to see if she landed the lie or not. They began walking to the house slowly. Rook was still in shock. He thought he'd never need to use those skills.

"They don't usually teach children," Rook said, "You must have been a special case." Nobody needed such fighting skills unless to subdue potentially violent mental patients. Then a thought occurred to him, *perhaps this is precisely why she was taught—her mother.*

Gwen didn't know if he believed her or not. His tone

said yes, his answer was skeptical at best.

She shrugged, "I don't know. It was a long time ago."

"You must have trained for a long time then. I can't imagine you'd forget the name of an art yet be dedicated enough to be so good at it."

Rook was skeptical and it showed on his face and in his tone. The guilt from lying to Rook began to seep in. She felt it sawing down through her center. *I can't keep this up much longer.*

"It's a long story and I would love to tell you about it some day—not today. I am truly sorry about your arm." Gwen desperately wanted to change the subject.

"It's nothing. I'm tough." He puffed out his chest and knocked on it with his fist, then laughed at himself.

Such a clown, she thought. Clown was not the right word—that sounded like an insult. *Character—that's the word I was looking for.* His antics were comical but in a subtle way. Not the annoying, ridiculous way she had seen others portray. Rook seemed to have just the right amount of humor, chivalry, sweetness, and sarcasm. Like a mixed drink made just to her taste—intoxicating just the same.

"So, what brings you down my street during the week at this time of the day? Aren't you supposed to be at the hospital? It's Thursday."

"No. It's Friday..." he said confused.

Friday! How did I miss an entire day? Gwen wondered.

"I was wondering if you would like to go fishing with me?" Rook asked excitedly.

"Um... I... uh... never tried it." A safe enough answer— not a complete lie. She had been fishing with her grandfather many times—all catch and release. Truth was, she had never been fishing in Rook's world. She wasn't even sure if it meant the same thing since there was no need to hunt.

"Great! I know the perfect place." The back-lit gray of

his eyes seemed to flicker or brighten with excitement.

Gwen eyed him suspiciously and thought, *I remember what happened the last time we went to 'the perfect place'.*

"Will we need to stop off and get the proper gear?" she asked.

"Nah. They have stuff there we can use and they'll know what the fish are partial to right now."

So he 'is' talking about fish. "Are fish picky?" she asked prying for more information—curiosity beginning to gnaw at her.

"Yeah, you could say that. Fish are like any other living creature—they get bored. If it isn't exciting, they won't play," he explained. He spoke as if he knew a great deal about fishing in this world.

Play with fish? Grandma always told me not to play with my food, her mind joked. "You fish a lot?" she asked.

He slowed his pace, silently gazing at the ground. "Not in a while." His tone grave. She regretted asking as soon as she realized she had struck a nerve. "Not since..." He trailed off.

Gwen finished apologetically, "The accident—I am so sorry."

Suddenly he was upbeat again—on the exterior. "You didn't know. How could you? And besides, I don't want you to hold anything back. Ask me anything you like, whenever you like." He smiled but his eyes remained glum.

Gwen was quickly learning what Rook's *tells* were. Everybody had them and she wondered, in this world, in this body, what hers were.

"I bet you are very good at what you do. I love this car," Gwen complimented as they drove away.

"It's probably not all that visible to the untrained eye but I tweaked a few things in the electromagnetic boosters," he boasted.

Her eyebrows pulled back. She had no idea what Rook was talking about and she watched him fight the urge to carry on with more technical car-talk. "I won't bore you with the details," he said taking notice to her facial expression.

"I doubt that you could ever bore me," she replied with a smile. "If you say something I don't want to hear, I'll just tune you out," she added bluntly.

A sudden look of shock hit his face, "Wow! I don't think I've ever heard such blunt honesty in my life and you're the last person I would expect it from."

"Do I seem like the dishonest type?" she asked mildly offended.

"Not at all. You seem so gentle and kind. Like you would hold back to spare someone's feelings."

"Strike one," Gwen joked. "I don't believe in lying. I realize that sometimes it's necessary in order to protect secrets, but other than that it is coward's play."

"Do you have any secrets?" Rook asked in a joking but deeply intrigued tone.

"I have a lot of secrets!" Gwen rolled her eyes as she thought of the overwhelming pile of secrets she had from him alone. She had been doing her best not to stack any more on top. Lying to Rook felt like the worse kind of betrayal, which made no sense to her."

"You are a government agent aren't you?" he joked, "Some sort of super spy. I saw those mad crazy skills!"

Rook got *so* into his little skits. Gwen looked forward to them. She thought he'd make a good actor—not just because he was beautiful enough for the big screen, but whatever he was doing at any given moment, he fully dedicated himself to. She detected it rolling off him and onto her delicate empathic senses—Rook had a passion for life that Gwen had never known before and would not likely see again in anyone else—his uniqueness was unfathomable.

This entire experience could be all in my head. It does run in the family. Well, who says you can't enjoy insanity? So far, insanity has welcomed me with far more open arms than the real world ever has. Gwen soaked in the glory of this other world for only a brief moment—it wasn't long before thoughts of her grandparents resurfaced. *I wonder what they are doing, while I'm off on this mental vacation.* She tuned back in to Rook's theories.

He is full of crazy ideas. Thankfully all the wrong ideas. Gwen just smiled and snickered at his accusations.

To Gwen, the water appeared no less glorious than anything else in this world. Her expectations were beginning to rise for all new experiences, and she had yet to be disappointed. A part of her hoped she would find disappointment soon. Anything to make her want to leave this place would help her for when that time came, if it ever came.

"You're going to have to show me how to do this you know?" Gwen said smiling, pretending to look dumbfounded by the fishing contraption. She had a good idea how it worked but was not prepared for the fishing experience of her life.

Sailboats, kayaks, canoes, and rowboats made use of the lake but nobody else was fishing. She began fantasizing about a romantic rowboat ride in the moonlight with Rook then shook the idea from her head. *No moonlit nights in this world, Gwen.* As if *that* were the unrealistic part of the fantasy. Some of the simplest pleasures of home were impossible in this perfect world.

"Why aren't any of the boaters fishing?" This seemed like a normal question to Gwen.

Rook's expression asked if she were serious. "You certainly haven't been fishing before," he said shaking his head and smiling—obviously enjoying a thought he didn't share.

"I told you," she replied incredulously.

Rook described the basics of casting and waiting then he turned the ends of the lures—they wiggled and lit up. *Oh man, Whinny would love this thing!*

"You got it?" Rook asked unsure.

"Yeah. I think so," Gwen replied sarcastically.

"Let's see it," Rook challenged.

Gwen was a little suspicious that he didn't throw the first cast. She cast her line out a good eight feet.

"Wow! Great cast! You're a natural," he praised.

Gwen let him massage his man-ego as he taught her how to fish.

"Now, just let it sit out there until you see it go under." Rook looked excited and anxious. *What a gentleman—allowing me to catch the first fish.*

Gwen's eyes widened in awe as large and small fish began leaping out of the water around her lure. A giant fish leaped four feet into the air and came down, mouth open, right on top of her lure. Her reflexes took over and she locked a grip on the fishing pole. "Hold your feet..." Rook warned, but not soon enough.

She went face-first into the water, still holding the pole. Rook grabbed her feet before the fish could pull her in further. The fish jumped out of the water with the lure in its mouth. *The fish is laughing at me!* Gwen thought angry. She was sure she heard it laugh.

Rook seized the fishing pole so she could get back on her feet. He laughed as he dug the heels of his feet into the dirt, pulling, and reeling in the large fish. He gave the line some slack and then began pulling and reeling again—a challenging tug-a-war match. He reeled the fish all the way in and held it up, clipped a scale to the end of a loop on the lure. "5 units! Not bad!" Rook gave Gwen an approving look.

"Alright little buddy, it's time to go back in. Thanks for playing. You're one heck of a fighter," Rook spoke to the fish and then dipped him back in the water with the lure. The fish let go and swam away.

"You knew that was going to happen didn't you?" Gwen asked with a semi-acidic playful tone.

"I didn't know, but I thought it would be an interesting surprise," he defended.

"You could have warned me! That was incredible! I thought it was going to yank my shoulders out of socket."

"Do you want to go?" Rook asked sincerely.

"No. This is fun! Anything else I should know before I cast this thing back out there?"

"Not that I can think of."

"How about you throw the next one?" Gwen suggested.

His eyes were a bright flow of gray, black and silver again—secretly Gwen's new favorite color combination.

"Fair enough," he said repressing a chuckle as he

smiled.

She was going to let it slide but couldn't help herself. "What? Something amusing? Besides the fact that I got muscled by a fish?"

Rook turned to face her sincerely—without humor. He reached to place his hand against her cheek and used his thumb to brush the dirt off—his fingers were warm and smooth against her hairline. The core of her soul spun and began to funnel inward. *I wish I could pause this moment and savor it forever,* she thought breathlessly.

"You have mud on your face and your soaked like a wet dog," he smiled. "It's cute."

"I don't smell like a wet dog do I?" she asked still breathless. She would have felt self-conscious but was too preoccupied with the funnel cloud spinning within her center.

Rook leaned in to smell her hair—closing the gap between them. The heat of his closeness, and his soothing scent made the funnel cloud spin faster. The gravity of her center multiplied exponentially. Her heart felt like it would leave bruises on the inside of her rib-cage from pounding so hard. The feeling was addicting and she knew it wasn't good for her, but when in the moment, she didn't care. Nothing else mattered while in the midst of her *high*. As if logic couldn't penetrate the mind once emotion was engaged.

"Nope, you smell great—as usual."

Gwen blushed. "Your sense of smell must be messed up," she commented.

He sniffed the air. "No, it's fine." He sniffed her again. "You smell fine."

"Would you please stop smelling me. You're making me nervous," she laughed self-consciously.

Rook gave her some space and smiled. "I'm trying to figure you out." He cast his line out into the water. "On one hand you appear daring and light spirited but on the other hand, you seem seriously conservative."

This sent the cold sensation through her veins. She didn't want him trying to figure her out—not yet. She needed to figure things out first. Gwen looked down at the ground unsure what to say next.

"I'm sorry. I didn't mean to sound so..."

"No, you're right. I'm flattered that you want to figure me out. I'm not used to that."

"I find that hard to believe," Rook said sincerely.

"Why? I'm no one special. Just a plain old girl."

"You're wrong," his voice was accusing and less relaxed then it had been, "There is something about you—something different—intriguing."

Gwen blushed and rolled her eyes to the side. "I'm glad you think so, but I'm beginning to think that you are easily amused."

"True. I do appreciate the small things in life. But that's irrelevant. The more I know about you, the more I want to know. You're like a good book."

"You don't know anything about me. I'll disappoint you. I'm not all that interesting—honestly." *If I'm a good book, I wonder what genre he'd find it under. Horror? Science Fiction?* she wondered.

"I disagree," he defended.

"You are so hard to reason with," Gwen teased.

"And you have that gift—the advantage with me—making me feel however you want. Just imagine how much I must frustrate everyone else."

Is that what I'm doing? Is he intrigued by me because I will it?

"You don't frustrate me. I find you just as intriguing."

He gave Gwen the skeptical *oh please* look.

"I'm serious! You mean you haven't noticed?" Gwen laughed humorlessly. "Are you blind? I know you're not stupid."

"What makes you so sure?" he joked.

"I'm *not* so sure anymore. Not after hearing how interesting you think I am," Gwen teased.

Rook chuckled. Gwen shook her head in awe at the conversation. *He finds me fascinating. I wonder how interesting he'd find me if he knew that I was, pretty much, an alien. A wardlow—whatever the heck that means.* She giggled quietly as she imagined the faces he would make at her.

Gwen closed her eyes, took in a few deep breaths, and reopened them before speaking, "Sometimes, I feel a sensation inside of me, like it's at the core of my being, like a force attempting to pull me inside out from my center." Gwen shaped her hands like she was holding a basketball out in front of her upper abdominal region.

Rook read accusation on her facial expression. "What? You think I have something to do with that?" he asked.

"Oh, I know you have something to do with it. I just wasn't sure if it was consciously or unconsciously—on your part." Gwen spoke in a matter-of-fact tone.

Rook stared through her as he thought about her description. "Unconsciously," he finally answered.

They continued fishing for two more hours. Gwen thought about how she would repay him for the mud-mask incident. They joked and laughed the entire time, which made hours pass like minutes. The moonlit day didn't allow them to forget time was almost up and they would, once again, have to part ways.

The fading light brewed sadness within them as they became increasingly inseparable. *Young love in this world is much more serious,* Gwen realized. She had no idea what she was weaving herself into. Worse yet she had no idea how much she was jeopardizing his innocence.

Gwen figured she would attempt the meditation to *induce the calm*—as Gwen calls it—while in the perfect darkness of Alexa's bed.

She began the countdown until the swirling colors settled. *This is new.* Her surroundings had a black and brownish-orange tint. *I am still in the house, but this looks more like home.* Gwen thought about being in her bedroom and suddenly she was there. She looked around her bedroom and saw herself, in Gwen-form, lying in bed. *What the heck is going on? Am I dreaming about the past? I'm sleeping in jeans and a tee-shirt. I don't remember ever doing that. I always wear my flannel pajamas.*

Gwen wondered if Grandma was still awake and suddenly found herself standing in front of the living room recliner where Bev was reading the paper. Gwen looked at the clock above the television set. *7:00 A.M.* Gwen tried to speak to her but couldn't make a sound. *She can't see me.* Bev set the paper down and reached for the remote control.

She's looking right through me, like I'm not even here. Gwen caught a glimpse of the newspaper, *current year—interesting.* The headline read: Alligator Escapes Detroit Zoo.

Gwen visualized the zoo and before she knew it, she was standing in the zoo where she noticed a fuzzy critter scared stiff staring at her. It looked like part of the monkey family. *I don't like this,* she thought. She focused on Bev's living room to see if she could appear there. It worked—she was back in the living room again. Rather than just appear from place-to-place Gwen decided to try walking. Her body felt like a single element—she was unable to move parts of her body independently. She attempted to move a leg forward but her entire body began gliding backward. So she tried moving backward instead which sent her gliding forward, toward the dining room.

Whinny lie on one of the dining room chairs. He turned his head. *He's looking right at me!* she thought. Like the strange monkey creature, it seemed as though he could see her. She tried to call to Whinny but once again couldn't make any sound. His ears perked up and he bounced off the chair onto the floor, in front of Gwen. He looked up at her and let out a short meow.

Bev heard the call. She turned toward the dining room and said, "Whinny? What's the matter? You hungry?" Whinny kept his eyes fixed on Gwen. His tail made an arced swoop across the linoleum floor once and then again. Bev made her way over to the kitchen to get some dry food for Whinny. "What are you staring at? Huh?" Bev followed his stare and looked passed Gwen. She was looking up at the wall behind her. She thought there might be a spider on the wall. Bev raised an eyebrow and shrugged. She topped off Whinny's food bowl and checked to see if he had fresh water.

Gwen reached out to touch Bev to see what would happen. Her hand passed right through her causing Bev to shiver—Gwen watched as chill bumps rose on her arms. Gwen reached out to pet Whinny but suddenly felt like she was gliding backward—away from him. It started out slowly but then in the blink of an eye, she was back in bed with her eyes closed. *Wow! What a rush!* Her mind foggy— speckles of white noise clouded her vision over-top of pitch blackness. *That trip was way better than the scary dark place! This time, no freaky nightmares either!*

Gwen jotted down the experience while the details were fresh in her mind: Inducing the Calm - start 10:30 P.M. end 10:45 P.M. *I'm sure I was conscious during the experience, unlike when I was dreaming.* Gwen looked at the clock—*Only 15 minutes? It seemed much longer than that. I covered a good amount of territory in 15 minutes! The experience was so real. Movement was a little awkward— backward. Navigation will take time and practice. Like a mirror image, everything felt backward.* Gwen wondered if she really stepped foot into her home world. *7:00 A.M. though? I began to induce the calm just short of 10:30 P.M. and when I returned it was 10:45 P.M.*

She lie in bed thinking of the endless possibilities until finally she drifted off to sleep.

Chapter Nine

Gwen walked into the auto shop and peeked her head into the garage. Rook was standing next to a red car on a hoist, speaking with a coworker—talking and making gestures toward the underside of a car. Rook saw her out of his periphery. His expression of contemplation turned to a smile as he walked over to greet her.

"Gwen! Is everything alright?" obviously trying to sound concerned first, and overjoyed second.

"Yeah. Great! We need to talk."

"I'm going to take my break now," Rook told Gus.

"You're out of here in about an hour anyway, go ahead and take off for the day. I can manage. We can work on this old beast tomorrow," Gus suggested.

"Well, I've got a few hours to spare, if you want to hang out at my place or something?" Rook suggested to Gwen.

"I was beginning to wonder if you lived at the shop. I'd love to check out your place."

During the five-minute drive to Rook's house, Gwen began telling him about the nightmare she had a few nights ago. He was so deep in thought that he passed the turn onto his street. "Tell me the rest when we get there. I would rather not pass by the house too," he said chuckling.

"So, what ya got going on in a few hours?" Gwen asked.

"Ah, it's nothing special, just a presentation at the College of Mechanics," Rook said modestly.

"That sounds pretty special to me. Aspiring students and potential future mechanics?"

"Yeah. I invented the battery-preserving technology most often used today. I did this as a student, and the faculty wants me to inspire them to think big."

"That's fantastic! I knew you were smart! I still question your judgment of character though," Gwen joked.

"Hey. You're going to give me a big head," Rook warned.

"Yeah. Your head is big enough as it is," she continued to joke.

Rook half-smiled—he was admittedly, a bit of a show-off. He liked that Gwen could joke openly about it, rather than turn away.

The enormous house on Haggerty and Nine Mile Road, though in mint condition, had an old allure it.

"Wow! Your house is huge. You could house a few families here if you wanted to."

"The same hands that built the stone building in the park," he said proudly.

"That's amazing. So, you have this all to yourself?"

"For now. Someday, I hope to raise a family here."

"A family? Or *your* family?" she teased.

He gave her that look again—her grandparents gave it to her as a child—an acknowledgment to her smart remark. His version of the look was more playful though. Gwen knew that if the roles were reversed, he would have said something similar.

"You planning on having a large family?" Gwen asked.

"I'm thinking much further ahead. I picture an old man and woman, surrounded by children and grandchildren.

We could have all of our holiday gatherings here."

Gwen liked the way he said *we*. Though she knew he didn't mean *he and her*. "You've got the yard for it." Gwen said as they walked to the door. There hung a wooden plaque with the family name carved into it. *Dresden—I could live with that*, she thought. *Gwen Dresden has a nice ring to it. It would eliminate the Penguin association to my maiden name. It rhymes too.* Gwen giggled at the thought.

"What?" Rook asked wary.

"Nothing," Gwen responded with mock innocence.

"You're going to make me feel insecure," Rook countered.

"Ha! I doubt that." She felt like a brat.

"I hate when you do that, you know," Rook said.

"I know," Gwen said with a sly smile.

He shook his head and quickly refocused on opening the door to welcome her into his family house.

The family room was to the left upon entering, stairs leading to the second floor directly in front of the entrance, a black iron guardrail lined either side of the steps, and across the front view of the second story—like a balcony. To the right, an entry into another large room— the living room. Gwen thought the old country feel, of the home, was as well portrayed inside as it was outside.

"Please, make yourself comfortable, I need to gather a few things for the presentation, and then you can tell me what's on your mind. I want to make sure that when the time comes, I can just grab my things and go."

"Sure. Where would you like me to wait?" Gwen looked in all directions of the large spaces on either side of her.

Rook gestured to the long room on the left.

"Okay, I will be on the couch then."

The room was even larger than it appeared from the doorway. The walls were decorated in artwork, family portraits and shelves where living plants stood. Though the house had a country feel, it also had the allure of old-world elegance. *I would have expected shades of gray to be a dreary scheme but it is anything but.*

She observed various family photos, which hung from the walls. *Nice to put faces to the names. A beautiful family, not surprising—everyone here is beautiful.* She had yet to see anything but beauty in this world. There hung a family portrait of Rook, Raven, and their parents. Most of the photos were of Rook and Raven at different stages in their lives. Raven was much smaller than Rook. No matter what age, he always had a few feet of height on her. Their happy expressions pained Gwen. The loss Rook felt for his little sister, was far worse than he allowed anyone to witness. Gwen saw their connection—the big protective brother bond clearly captured in time. His posture was different while near her—protective. Gwen spent the better part of her days, in this world, observing Rook's mannerisms and behavior. She became such the expert that oftentimes he accused her of having a secret mind-reading ability.

Rook sat quietly on the large couch behind where Gwen stood. He patted the seat next to him. "I thought you said you would be on the couch. Come sit and tell me what's on your mind."

Though the story would sound crazy, for the moment, Gwen thought it would be so easy to tell Rook about everything.

"Do you believe in out-of-body experiences?" she asked.

"I haven't put much thought into it but I guess anything is possible."

If he can accept this then maybe it won't be such a stretch to believe the rest, she hoped.

"I think I experienced one last night," she explained.

"Wow! Really? What was it like?"

"Strange but not unlike the experience I had with you in the sanctuary—only this was not scary."

"Do you believe in multiple realms of existence?" Gwen asked hoping she wasn't pushing her luck.

"Hmm—I guess it's possible. Is that what you are going to tell me next? That you went to another world?" Rook asked with a semi-skeptical expression on his face, which made Gwen nervous.

"Not exactly," she paused to think of where to start next. "You are the only one I have and I need you to trust me. I can't figure this out alone," Gwen pleaded.

Rook nodded. Gwen said she needed him and that made his soul sore like a bird.

Gwen considered his possible reactions, some good, some bad.

She had to resist all urges to continue the story, deep down, she really wanted him to hear. He was taking everything so well. *I am too comfortable with him for my own good.* Her heart was in a constant tug-of-war match with her mind. Emotion versus logic. The left brain versus the right brain. *If I were in Gwen-form I would surely have gone mad by now.* The scary part was, she was drawn to this feeling. She was like a cutter—a person who cuts themselves repeatedly claiming that the physical pain numbs his or her inescapable deep emotional pain. Gwen's self-inflicted wounds, numb now, would catch up to her later like a high-interest, credit card bill at the end of the month after a ridiculously frivolous shopping spree. Fully aware of the consequences she continued to involve herself with him. *I have never been so selfish in my life!*

"What's the matter? You're zoning out on me," Rook asked concerned.

"Oh—was I?" she snapped out it.

"I just realized that we need a longer block of time for this conversation."

I do have other, more sane, conversation I could have with him. "I was wondering," she hesitated to continue, "do you have any friends? I mean, the only reason I ask is because you are always with me, working or at the hospital."

"Oh I don't mind a bit. I have friends, but not like I used to. Since the accident, my friends don't know how to act around me. If they showed pity, it upset me, if they don't, it upset me. I distanced myself from them for quite some time and eventually, they just quit calling and coming around. We cross paths every now and again. It isn't awkward or anything. I just don't have the same priorities since the accident."

"I know exactly what you mean," she said sympathetically.

"Do you?" Rook gave her a look as if to check her sincerity.

"Maybe not exactly, but I do know what it's like to lose someone, and I had the same problem with *my* friends. Oh, and before I forget, I found my phone, I wanted to give you the number," she said reaching into her pocket.

"Are we not past the *exchanging of phone numbers* stage?" he asked jokingly.

"Well, I suppose; we did bolt rather quickly to the *hey, wanna wear my ring?* stage," she joked back.

"I didn't say you *had* to wear it, just that you *could*," he smiled.

"How would you have felt if I didn't?" Gwen arched an eyebrow curiously.

Instead of answering he asked, "so what stage are we in now?"

She heard her heart pounding as it blasting against her rib-cage. She had been asking herself the same question but didn't want to be the one to define their relationship. *What if he didn't view our time together, the way I did? I could ruin everything. Words are much more powerful than people often give them credit for.*

"I was just about to ask you the same thing," she said attempting to put the ball back in his court. She was afraid to look into his eyes just then. Afraid of how she would react if his words ripped her heart into pieces. She didn't want to see the deadly blow coming. On the other hand, if he were about to tell her he felt the same, she would have better self-control, if not paralyzed by his intoxicating gaze. The moment felt like disarming an explosive—deciding which wire to cut and then waiting for the outcome, while hesitatingly snipping the wire. The explosive was strapped to her heart and she felt the timer counting down with every beat. Once he snipped the wire, her heart would either stop beating, or explode. She wasn't sure which wire would result in which scenario. These were the only two possibilities she could fathom for the moment. To Gwen, time seemed to be moving impossibly slow. She expected to hear a talk-show host say, "your results—after the break."

Rook was so quiet that Gwen had to turn to look at him to be sure he didn't dozed off or have a stroke.

"Hey, are you day-dreaming?" she asked tapping her wrist.

"Sorry about that," Rook replied.

Rook snapped out of it wide-eyed, "Shoot! What time is it?"

He looked at the clock above the fireplace. "I hate to cut our time short, but we have to get going. I wish I didn't have this presentation today."

Saved by the bell. I hope the car ride won't be awkward, Gwen thought.

Rook looked forward to driving Gwen home. Riding in the car somehow fueled his confidence.

"So, are you sick of me yet?" Rook asked.

Gwen smiled at Rook and joked, "I'm surviving," she chuckled, "And you?"

"Oh, I am so sick of me," he said chuckling. They laughed together.

"I'd like to see you again later if you think you can tolerate me," he said.

"Well, I'd have to reschedule my plan of moping around the house and doing nothing—hmm... done." Gwen loved how easy it was to joke with him. She felt like she could talk to him for days straight, if not, weeks or even years. She wondered if it were better to savor these moments, or try to forget them. *This isn't going to end well,* her conscience warned.

"So, how soon can you rescue me from self-boredom?" she asked.

"About three hours."

"That should be enough time," she said.

Rook displayed confusion on his face. "Enough time for what? To get bored?"

"No. I have a surprise for you."

"A surprise?" Rook asked amused, "What's the occasion?"

"Oh I don't know—putting up with me, saving my life, just because. You pick. It doesn't matter to me."

"You don't owe me anything. I should be surprising

you. I have been so miserable for these last two years—in fact—I didn't realize how miserable until I met you. It's you who saved my life!"

Flattery and guilt rushed Gwen simultaneously. *It's amazing this body is capable of feeling conflicting emotions simultaneously—something I won't miss.*

Just before she got out of the car, she pulled her phone number from her pocket and gave it to him. She didn't want to offer it any earlier for fear that he would ask her where they stood in their friendship—or—whatever it was. A part of her wanted nothing more than to have everything out on the table—letting the cards fall as they may. Another part of her was afraid to know and wanted the fantasy to continue undiminished. Gwen kept playing this mad game of emotional tug-of-war with herself and worried her personality might just rip into multiple versions of herself.

As soon as Gwen stepped into the house, the phone rang with a picture of Cat displayed on the screen.

"Hello?"

"Where are you?" Cat asked.

"Right now, I'm home. I'm going to Rook's house in a few hours to hang out."

"Okay. Good. I'm coming by tomorrow to get you. Don't make any plans."

"Not a problem. I'll see you then." Gwen hung up the phone, surprised the conversation with Cat was so short and uncomplicated. *Must be the phone issue—the lines aren't clean. This reminded her of a high-tech spy movie.*

Gwen knew exactly what to do with her spare time. She hoped to have the painting for Rook done before their next visit. *Shouldn't take more than a few hours,* she thought.

The doorbell rang. Gwen welcomed the disturbance plopping down the brush before walking to the door.

Suddenly, she thought about her close encounter with the khaki man. Her steps slowed, but continued. There was knocking now. She thought the wrapping sounded was too small to be the khaki man and then she heard Cat's voice. Gwen took in a deep sigh of relief as she stepped faster. Gwen swung the door open.

"Cat! I thought we weren't getting together until tomorrow. Why didn't you tell me you were coming over? We just got off the phone! I wasn't expecting you and you scared the heck out of me!"

"I know. I know. I'm sorry. It's just that I wanted to give you something."

"Well, come on in. I need to ask you a very simple question anyway." They sat across from one another on the couches.

Cat pulled something out of a bag she was carrying and tossed a small book on the table, toward Gwen. It had a little weight to it as it plopped onto the glass table, and slid about 5 inches. Gwen grabbed it from the table for closer examination. It had a dark olive-green cover—the material resembled flattened out bamboo leaves. It had a combination lock on the side like a diary and was just a little bigger than a deck of cards, but two-to-three inches thick. The binding appeared to be well broken in. The pages looked to be brown, or trimmed in brown the way the bible was trimmed in gold.

"What am I supposed to do with this?"

"I don't know. Alexa gave it to me about a month or two ago. I thought it might be a clue," Cat said. "So what's your simple dilemma?"

"I'm working on a painting—a gift—for the guy I told you about. Well, I'm having trouble with it."

"You're the artistic one. Not me," Cat said shrugging.

"It's not *that* kind of a problem. Occasionally, I paint pictures at home. Alexa paints these fabulous paintings. So, why are my brushstrokes so sloppy?" she sounded defeated as she explained to Cat.

Cat looked confused. "I'm not sure if I can help you. Let's have a look at this work of art."

"Well, there's your problem!" Cat's tone triumphant.

Gwen paused mid-brushstroke—staring perplexed at the picture.

Cat pulled the brush out of Gwen's right hand and placed it in her left. "Try that!" Gwen thought she detected Cat rolling her eyes.

"Wow! I'm left-handed now!" Gwen's eyes were as big as saucers elated by how swiftly her hand cooperated with her now. "This is amazing!"

"We are *all* left-handed," Cat said.

"Really? That is *so* interesting. In my world, we are one or the other—predominately right-handed though some people can even use both hands equally."

"See. It's simple things like that which we don't know—relevant or not—we just don't know.

"I'll be happy to tell you anything you want to know. Actually, I'm pretty excited about our meeting tomorrow."

"I will pick you up. Don't make any plans for the day, Cat reminded Gwen. How is your guy friend doing? Is he still clueless?"

"Yeah." She shifted her glance to the floor as she hung on the end of the word.

"What? What is it?" Cat's pulse quickened.

"It's hard to lie to him," Gwen said still looking at the floor, feeling ashamed of her weakness.

"You have to! Do not blow this! Of all the possibilities Alexa foreseen—some were really out there—this was not one of them. I should have been there with you. I should have been there when you went down, and this variable would not exist."

Gwen's stomach ached at the thought of never having met Rook.

Cat vented her frustration, "I don't know what Alexa thinks she will accomplish once all is said and done but I hope it's worth it. She had better not get us all executed by the grand jury!"

"You mean. You hope *I* don't get us all killed! This is in *my* hands now? Is *that* what is at stake here?" Gwen was on the edge of hyper-ventilation. She stormed out of the art room and back to the living room couch. "How much time do I have to figure this out?" Gwen yelled.

Cat chased after Gwen and sat next to her on the couch. She put her hand on Gwen's shoulder to calm her down. "You're not alone in this. I'm so sorry you had to be collateral damage in this, but we have been working on this for a while. Innocent people are being executed. It has to stop before things get worse."

"How long do we have?" Gwen asked. She *really* wanted to know how much time she had left with Rook. Gwen's head spun. *This is 'so' much worse than I thought.*

"I'm not sure. It could be weeks, it could be months. From my understanding—which isn't much—we should be looking at a month minimum and three months maximum."

"There is so much that doesn't make sense! So much about your world is the same: the way you measure time, the language you speak, even some of the slang you use. It makes me think I'm insane! This is so impossible you know?" Gwen exclaimed.

"Believe me, I know. When Alexa first told me her theories, I thought it was impossible too. But once Alexa gets something in her head it's impossible to stop her."

"Sounds like I have big shoes to fill. I hope she isn't disappointed," Gwen said. "I'm scared. Just the other day, there was a man at my door, he sent chills down my spine, and I'm not even sure why," Gwen explained.

"A man? What did he look like?" Cat asked worried.

Gwen described the khaki man. As she described him she saw and felt Cat's demeanor change. Gwen sensed fear.

"What?"

"Hunters," Cat said aloud while thinking so much more. "Already?" Cat continued to work it out in her head.

"Dare I ask what they hunt?" *Please don't say wardlows. Please don't say wardlows.*

"Hunters search for wardlows. *Crap!* she thought. Her eyes tightened shut as she buried her face in her hands. *Man! If Rook had showed up five minutes sooner...*

"You need to do some homework. I will makes sure we bring any notes we have on them." Cat wasn't looking at Gwen anymore, she was deep in her own mind. "Alexa was right... you *can* see them." Cat's eyes brightened with the sudden realization. "That gives us the advantage. If she is right about that, then hopefully that means she really does know what she is doing."

"Do I want to know?" Gwen asked.

"Don't worry about it tonight. Enjoy this last night as yourself, because tomorrow, you will be the queen bee in our operation. Get some rest. Don't do anything stupid before tomorrow."

"I'm sure I can manage the rest of the day. I will have to let Rook know I can't see him tomorrow."

Cat didn't comment but it was easy to see how little

significance Rook played in the battle-plan. *It's for the best. He can come to his own heartbreaking conclusions when I stop seeing him. Lives depend on my actions and I certainly couldn't live with his blood on my hands. What have I done? I have got to try and fix this.*

Gwen took advantage of her time alone and was surprised at how well the painting took her mind off of the impending doom on the horizon.

Chapter Ten

"So, how did your presentation go?" Gwen asked as she sat on Rook's cozy couch.

"It went well. Thank you for asking. There were more students than my last presentation," Rook said amused.

"That's great!" Gwen wondered how she was able to stay so calm under the circumstances.

"So did you have enough time to get bored?" Rook joked.

"Not entirely. I am working on something. It's a surprise."

"You play?" Gwen asked pointing to the guitar hanging on the wall.

"Not so much anymore. Well, not the way I used to—not for fun," Rook added.

"It's something Raven and I did together. She loved to sing along. We wrote songs together. Some were funny, others more serious. It just depended on the mood and, of course, how much thought and preparation we put into it."

Rook was half-smiling, his expression lightened ever so slightly as a memory surfaced. A good memory, Gwen guessed. The memory made his soul center ache the way cheeks ache when eating something sour.

"Did *you* write or sing at all?" Gwen asked treading lightly on the topic. She envisioned an *Adam Sandler* style lyric.

"Some—but not as much as Raven. There is one old song that I still play, which I wrote for her. I play it for her every Thursday. She was always fond of the music but never wrote any lyrics for it. She said that it was too good to just throw any old vocals to. She didn't want to distract from the flow of the music. When it came to music, Raven was beyond her years. It was easy to forget you were talking to a child. This song was special to her for some reason. To me, it was just another tune I threw together." Rook paused in thought, "I can't remember her taking any other song so seriously."

"Wow! So, tomorrow?"

"Yep. I will pack up the acoustic and play the song at her bedside along with a few others."

"Will you play something for me? If it's not too painful, that is," Gwen asked hopeful.

"I'm a little rusty," Rook said modestly. "I haven't sang in front of open eyes in long time."

"I don't mind. I won't laugh or anything. I promise," Gwen assured him.

"This is an instrumental I wrote about five years ago. I kept this one to myself. I guess that makes it *your* song now," he said sentimentally, "I hope you like it."

She listened in awe as he played *her* song. *I wish I could hear him sing.* She didn't want to push her luck by asking. Gwen loved the rich tone of the acoustic guitar. Her new ears allowed her to appreciate the depth of that richness now. The sound radiated through her soul center reactivating the magnetic pulling sensation.

"Wow! Rook, that was so awesome! You should be sharing your talent with others! Your music makes me feel something I've never felt before," she said excitedly.

"It's nothing. I don't like the idea of others critiquing my music the way people always do. Good or bad—I don't think anyone should be allowed to judge what's in my soul."

"I guess that makes sense. Well, I hope you don't mind

me telling you how awesome and absolutely beautiful your soul is." Her mouth got away from her again, and out came the words she would have rather kept to herself. She blushed.

"I don't mind at all. Thank you."

"I'd like to hear you sing sometime," she encouraged.

"Nah! You don't want to hear that," he said placing the guitar back on the wall-hook."

"Oh yes I would! I bet you have the voice of an angel," she insisted.

His smile was accented by the flushing of his cheeks. "You sound like my mom."

"Oh. Sorry." Gwen didn't want to drag down the moment with touchy subjects.

"Don't be. It's a good thing. My mother gave me all the support and self-confidence I could ever need. She would get us all together, as a family, so that Raven and I could perform every week. It didn't matter if we were improvising, or they were were songs she heard a thousand times. It was a way for us to spend quality time together as a family. I will always cherish my memories of the time we had together."

"What about your father?" Gwen asked curiously.

"He was supportive too. A mother's bond is something special though. Don't get me wrong, I love my father with all my heart, but Mom and I were like twin souls—we had a special connection. Whenever something was wrong with one of us, the other knew it. I'll never forget the precise moment when the accident happened. My senses fell away for a minute and then I felt something severe from within me. It felt like my left and right rib-cage collided with one another. It scared me out of my skin! I felt a hollow spot within my heart like something had just ripped a chunk out of my chest, leaving me short of breath. I panicked and suddenly I was pacing back and forth trying to figure out what to do next. I wanted to rush home but suddenly I was unsure if I could spell my name, much less, find my way home. It wasn't home that drew me anyway. I followed my instincts to the hospital. I was there before my family arrived. I knew it was bad but I wasn't sure just how bad. Mom didn't make it alive. I sensed the emptiness before leaving for the hospital—like a chunk ripped from my soul —and so I doubted she was alive much past closing the doors to the ambulance. I saw them wheel my father and sister in. Then it was confirmed; I would never see my mother's smile again. She would never laugh at our performances again. She would never lay another warm hand of encouragement on my shoulder."

Rook caught his mood spiraling down and didn't want to fall apart, any further than he already had. "You said you were familiar with loss. Who was it?"

"I... don't think I'm ready to talk about it—not just yet. Please don't be offended. It's not that I don't trust you, it's just that I'm not sure I could get the words out and I am already in agony from absorbing your pain. I'd rather not add to it."

"I understand," Rook said. He was disappointed but didn't want to show it.

"I promise to tell you about it. I want to tell you about it. My wounds are just as fresh as yours. It was only a few years ago. I admire your ability to cope the way you have. I wish I were as strong as you. Just one of the things I admire so much about you," Gwen complemented.

Rook arched his eyebrow in response to her comment. She was frustrated by how effortlessly he tugged at her puppet-strings and how willing she was to give him whatever he wanted. Feeding him the answers he sought, was a real addiction for her—something of a power-trip.

"You know what? You just spilled your heart out to me and hearing myself speak just now, I realize I'm being completely selfish. I *will* tell you. I had one true friend with whom I trusted every detail of my life. She was like a sister to me."

Gwen's sense of emptiness was overwhelming. She felt like her insides were melting. She thought it would have been enough to make her cry, as her eyes begin to heat up, but the tears didn't come.

"Another long story?" Rook gave her that semi-sarcastic smile.

This smile combined with his irresistibly magnetic eyes got to her every time. *Could he know this weakness exists within me? The pulling probably isn't so bad, but I forget to breathe sometimes. It's no wonder I get dizzy while we are eye-locked.*

"I have only spoke about this with one other person and that was a long time ago, under a confidentiality agreement," she cautioned.

"I'm flattered to have gained your trust so easily," Rook smiled sincerely.

"You should be. You are a special case," Gwen replied.

Jokingly Rook replied, "I'm special."

Gwen's laughter surprised her. No matter how subtle, Rook always managed to find her funny-bone. The sensation tickled her from under her rib-cage. *I will miss this when I return home to my laughter-less, mundane life.*

"Okay short-bus, I'll tell you my tragic little story," she joked.

"I am so slap-happy when we are together," she added.

"Me too," Rook agreed.

Gwen's heart tripped over itself in her chest. Rook had a knack for catching her off-guard. He could stop all of her thought processes simultaneously, changing their direction into one primary focus of his choice. She was glad that he had a way of breaking the tension. *A precious gift,* she thought. This slap-happy moment gave her enough of a break from the emotion of Rook's tragic story so she could tell hers. Gwen thought this might have been intentional.

Rook wanted her to realize he had something more to offer than gloom and doom. Gwen had been a God-send as far as Rook was concerned. He needed someone he could relate to, and he believed deep in his core that this odd girl was that person.

"This is very hard for me to talk about, please bear with me." Gwen closed her eyes and took a few deep breaths.

"I swore I would never let myself get close to anyone again. My dreams of future relationships, friends, social gatherings, getting married, having children—all of that died with her. She was my best friend. We considered ourselves sisters rather than friends. We did everything together. There were no secrets between us. We talked about what it would be like when we were older. How we would go off to college together, double-date and one day we would walk the aisle. She would be my maid of honor, and I hers—an arrangement set in stone. We agreed to never let any boy come between us. Any *big* decision, either of us faced, was discussed before finalized. We were each others lifeline."

"We planned to go to Paris, take pictures and see all of the major tourist attractions, especially the paintings and sculptures. Baylee was a huge art buff. She was very artistic herself—enough to earn a full scholarship to an accredited art school.

We finally got the opportunity to take the trip during

spring break of our sophomore year. This trip would knock off one of the big plans on the extensive *to do* list. We were so excited about the trip; it was all we talked about for a month prior. We even came up with make-believe scenarios of how we would be swept off our feet by Mr. Right.

Our scenarios almost always got out of hand, and we would laugh so hard that our ribs hurt for two days. Our rib muscles were probably super buff after years of this. No one made me laugh the way Baylee could. I have never laughed so hard with anyone else—until I met you. To laugh at all, usually brings back memories of her. When I think of something funny, it's a reflex to wonder what Baylee would say if she were with me."

"I came down with the stomach flu the day before our flight was scheduled. At first we thought it might be nerves because I'd never flown before. I didn't want to miss the trip and I know she didn't want to go without me. This was something we were supposed to do together. I told her that no matter what, she should go without me. This trip meant more to her. I didn't want to be the anchor holding her back from her dreams. Now, of course, I wish I had."

Gwen closed her eyes and swallowed hard, "I convinced her to go. If I asked her to, she would have postponed the trip. I know she would have."

"That night, I was so sick and so weak that I knew I wouldn't make the trip. I felt like I was going to die on the bathroom floor and I wanted to at one point. I was so sick! I had a 104 degree fever and my body ached. My head pounded and I tossed and turned all night. I had a nightmare that the plane crashed into the ocean. I attributed the nightmare to my guilt for not going and anxiety about flying over the ocean. I wished I would have seen it for what it was. I should have called her and begged her not to get on that plane. She would have listened to me. I know she would have. I could have saved her life!"

"The day after she took flight, I was so exhausted from being sick, I slept through the following two days. I was eating a bowl of oatmeal with apple slices and walnuts when I saw the headline in the news—*Plane Missing.* The pit of my stomach sank. I knew it was her plane. The sinking feeling paralleled the feeling I had upon waking from the nightmare. The sinking feeling then, paired with the nausea and exhaustion, was harder to detect for what it was. Had I not been sick with the flu—maybe I would have prevented the trip or, maybe I would have been convinced it was anxiety and have been on that plane too."

"Remnants of the plane were eventually found along with the black box. It was confirmed that the plane was mangled by a severe thunderstorm. The winds mangled the plane. No survivors nor bodies were recovered. But this didn't surprise me, given the nature of where the plane crashed. The passengers became shark food. They would be bleeding and unconscious when they hit the water. Those who didn't drown, were killed before hitting the water, or eaten alive. I try not to think about which fate Baylee suffered. One of *her* biggest fears was drowning and I just can't imagine how horrified she must have been once she realized her worst nightmare had come true."

Gwen noticed Rook's perplexed look and sensed that he had something to add or a question to ask. "What?"

"I don't want to sound stupid and I'm sure it's probably not a relevant part of your story so forgive me for asking, but you lost me with the eating thing? Did I misunderstand? What is oatmeal?"

Gwen realized she had let her guard down and was speaking on autopilot. *Dang it! It was bound to happen. I got complacent.* Gwen wondered just how much he failed to understand.

"What's the matter?" Rook panicked.

Gwen put her forehead in her hands and rested her elbows on her knees. *I can't bring him into this! He doesn't deserve it. I've been so selfish!*

"I'm sorry if you felt like you had to tell the story," Rook said sympathetically.

Gwen didn't have the strength to look him in the eyes yet.

"Let's talk about something else," Rook suggested.

"I don't know who I am." Gwen blinked, swallowed and attempted to put things in better perspective. "I mean, I know who I used to be. But..."

Rook interrupted, "If you've done something in the past I'm sure it's not that bad. I'm here for you," he said sitting beside her to pat her knee. "Now spill it," he insisted.

"It's not that simple!" she said getting up from the couch, shaking her hands out stiffly in front of her face in frustration. She felt like pulling her hair out.

This conversation was torture for both of them. She stood with her back to him to avoid locking eyes with him in this frustrated state-of-mind. Then she stood with her back against the wall and slid to the floor. She interlaced her fingers in her hair, she rested her face in the palms of her hands.

Rook walked over to her, knelt down to eye-level placing his hand on her shoulder. He lifted her chin forcing her to look him in the eyes. She took notice of the serious look on his face now. She *had* to tell the truth when he looked at her that way. She wondered if he saw through her eyes into the depths of her soul. She feared if he caught her lying she couldn't bear the disappointment on his face. She certainly couldn't bear the thought of losing his trust.

He spoke calmly, "I don't care what you've done. Nothing is going to change the connection we have—the connection I felt from the first time our eyes locked. The fact that you are so reluctant to tell me, whatever it is, makes me wonder if the connection is a one-way street. I assumed that I could only feel such a connection with someone who felt the same—an unobstructed flow of energy between us. If you felt for me the way I do for you, you would know there is nothing you can say to change that."

Gwen was overwhelmed by his proximity: his hand was on her, his eyes locked on hers, and his words sent an ocean of warmth swirling around inside of her. She was dizzy from his words. *He does feel he same for me,* she thought. A part of her wanted to believe it, another thought it would be easier if she didn't.

"I do feel the same connection, which is why I am so afraid. I don't think I can stand to be without you."

She wanted to wrap her arms around him and reassure him.

Rook stood up, offered Gwen his hand so he could pull her up off the floor. She got to her feet but Rook didn't release her hand. They sat on the couch together, facing one another. He wrapped his fingers in hers, and put his free hand on top. She put her free hand on his. They locked eyes.

A moment passed and neither spoke a word. She could stay like this forever and it wouldn't matter if they ever spoke another word. Though she couldn't read his mind— and she was sure he couldn't read hers—it seemed like words were a less sufficient tool for communicating their feelings in this very moment. Gwen had no words to describe their connection. Soul-mate, twin flame, true love —none of these did her feelings justice.

I can't keep this from him any longer. She closed her eyes, took a deep breath and when she reopened them she began:

"I went to sleep as Gwen Penn, and awoke as Alexa Murdock."

He sighed and said, "Okay, I'm not sure what you mean. You are going to have to speak more literal than that."

"I meant every word literally." Gwen gave him a moment to rerun the words back in his head before continuing.

"Rook! I am a wardlow!" Gwen finally spit the words out, closed her eyes bracing herself for his reaction.

Her eyes opened wide in shock as she heard Rook laugh loudly.

"You really got me this time. You're good. You should think of writing live shows." Rook still roaring with amusement. A wardlow," he chuckled. The things you come up with," he added. Frustrated Gwen thought, *Oh, he is not going to make this easy!*

Her serious expression lightened as she watched Rook laugh harder than she's ever seen him laugh before. *Well, that wasn't the reaction I was expecting. Maybe now is not the time. Hey, I tried to tell him. It's not my fault he doesn't believe me,* she justified.

Her mood changed in a heartbeat, "We may not see much of each other after tomorrow."

Rook was stunned, "What? Why not?"

"A friend of mine tracked me down the other day," she said while wondering how she was going to pull off this half-truth. "We have this study group. Unfortunately, since my memory-loss, I don't remember much, so they are all going to try and cram me full of information."

"What are you studying?"

"Honestly, I'm not really sure." *Back to lying,* she thought. "All I know is, it's a big deal and I play an important role, and there isn't much time left until the project deadline."

Rook's disappointment filled the atmosphere of the room. This is the moment he had been worried about—the day her friends find her—she would return to memories of a former life. He had no idea how literal that possibility was.

"Tomorrow is my first meet with the group. I don't know when we'll be able to hang out again." She sighed and couldn't look him in the eye so she opted to look to the floor instead. "It's probably better that we don't see each other any more."

Rook felt as though the wind had been knocked out of him. "What! Why?" he reached for the tops of her arms. "Look me in the eyes and say it. I don't believe you! You *just* said..."

Her eyes burned, yearning for tears that wouldn't come. She raised her head up to face Rook keeping her eyes closed. Unable to look him in the eyes she interrupted, "I know what I said! I can't..."

"Because you don't believe it!" Rook let go of her and turned away from her, pacing the room. He didn't want her to see him like this. He wasn't prepared for her sudden rejection. They were having too much fun together. They were too perfect for each other. It just made sense. "I won't force myself on you. I won't beg for your acceptance. I care for you, and I guess," He took a moment to think before speaking, "I should have expected it." He put the palm of his hand against his eyes and forehead, pushed it back through his creatively chaotic hair, "I'm not meant to be happy."

Gwen was heartbroken for having caused him such heartache. She approached him from behind and put a hand on his back and the other on his arm. She sensed that he didn't want her to see his face right now, so she didn't insist. Gwen preferred not to get trapped in his gaze right now anyway. "I care for you," she paused—treading the subject lightly—unsure how this world expressed such emotions, "I care for you too much. There are things in my life right now that I need to figure out."

Rook turned to face her now, with an expression of reassurance and determination, "I will help you."

"You won't. You don't know what your saying," Gwen said, her eyes widened in protest.

"I don't care. Whatever it is, I'm sure I can handle it, better than never seeing you again," he added.

"You don't understand! I can't explain! I'm so confused! I hate this!" Gwen yelled frustrated and torn with emotion. *Why can't I cry?* she screamed in her mind. "I'm just trying to do what's best for both of us."

"Can you see the future? Is that one of your special abilities?" Rook asked though he knew the answer.

"No."

"Well then, how can you say that?" he insisted.

"If you knew what I knew—which is not much at this point—you would understand."

"So tell me. Put me out of my misery. Scare me away if you think you can. Give it your best shot." Rook felt as if he were winning the argument.

"I am afraid I will repulse you. All I know for sure is that if we continue to see each other, we will both, inevitably, get hurt."

"Yea, because this," Rook said sarcastically, "is loads of fun! I think I will take my chances. Besides, don't I get a say in the matter?" Rook urged, offended by Gwen's assumption.

She turned her back on him and made her way over to his couch feeling defeated. Rook followed and sat by her side.

Rook put the palms of his hands on the outside of Gwen's interlaced hands. "Can we work this out somehow? I need you in my life now, more than ever. I know that sounds selfish but I don't really care. You need to know how I feel," Rook pleaded.

Her heartbeat felt heavy in her chest. "I will call you in a day or two. Don't forget that I warned you. I don't know if I can bear to be away from you for too long, I just know that it's the right thing to do. For now, we will agree to disagree."

She sat silently on his couch, accepting of his touch, mentally kicking herself for giving in. The pull of her center was uncomfortable while accompanied by such grief. *Maybe if I just let go—seriously tell him everything—I can be free.*

Chapter Eleven

Cat began the introduction, "Gwen, meet Brendon, Jazz, Pico, and Hui-ming."

"Is this it? The group?"

"These are the main players—the most trustworthy. Alexa will bring the rest into the loop once she returns. We can help you understand our kind. We have so much to learn from you. Interacting with you, plus whatever data Alexa brings back should be enough.

"What if it's not enough? Can we change places again in the future?"

"Not likely. We had only enough serum to induce one trip. The remaining sample is for research. The secret died with Dr. Murdock. Alexa has his records but we believe his serum was all created by accident. He was so into his work—Alexa gets that from him. We believe he never put it in writing, either because he thought he'd have time to later, or in case something bad happened to him in the process. He wouldn't want his work replicated."

"Let's get started, shall we?" Anxious to get moving, it felt as if time was slipping away far faster than it should. Gwen sat in a lone chair positioned in front of a large easel. The other five sat at a narrow rectangular table facing her.

"Great. Who wants to start?" Cat asked the small group. "I know we all have questions for Gwen, I can start if you like."

The four new faces in the group were in awe as they

watched Gwen closely—they hardly blinked. "I'll ask first," Cat finally said while standing in front of the seat on the end. "What differences have you noticed so far?"

Gwen's eyebrows rose in response to the list of things, which populated her mind so rapidly.

"Where to start?"

"Ah. One of the huge differences between our realities is that you are all nocturnal whereas, my people live throughout day and night. We eat and drink for nourishment."

Gwen read confusion on their faces. "The sun does not fuel our bodies. Too much of it can actually make us sick —it burns our skin."

A baby-faced boy with blond hair spoke, "What does the sun look like?"

"It's a large ball of light in the sky. Sometimes it looks orange and sometime it looks yellow. The sun's light is so bright that it will blind us if we look directly at it. White puffs in the sky, called clouds, sometimes float across the sky and block the sun but our days remain lit. When the sun is out, we see things similarly to the way you see when the moon is out, except that our sky is a different shade of blue. But when the sun sets, we see darkness. Not the same kind of darkness—our eyes adjust to some extent. We use man-made light during the night to see."

Questions of Gwen's observations continued for an hour. "Okay, how about you tell me what's going on and what I can do to help? Cat has told me very little about what is going on and from what I understand, my role is huge. So, my questions for you are:

How did I get here? Why am I here? What is a wardlow—exactly? What is it I am supposed to do?"

Pico began, "Alexa is head honcho around here. She keeps us in the dark on the most specific details. You are a synthetic wardlow—the switch was induced chemically.

We didn't know if it would work, therefore we aren't sure why it worked or if it worked at all."

"I am here, so it worked," Gwen said as if the answer was obvious.

"We cannot say for sure. That is to be determined," Hui-ming countered.

"What do you mean?" Gwen asked suspiciously.

"It is possible that Alexa/you are delusional and in your hunt for wardlow justice you are living the delusion of your expected outcome."

"I don't even know what a wardlow is. I have a life back home. One that I remember every detail of. Trust me, this is no delusion!"

"If that is what Alexa expected, it's possible you are her delusion," Hui-ming explained.

"That's insane! And impossible!" Gwen retorted defensively.

"You still question what's possible after all you have been through. That is a very strong Alexa-trait," Brendon suggested.

"You don't know what it's like! So, until you literally walk in someone else's shoes, I don't think you should judge," Gwen protested. She didn't expect to be a lab rat in some twisted experiment. "Does Alexa know how much faith you put in her? She is the expert right? She is the one with enough 'nads to embark on the journey!"

"Your defensiveness for her is suspicious. You don't know her apart from any of us."

"You aren't judging her right now! You are judging me! If this is all that I come to learn, I'm leaving. I did not come here to be put on trial. I can't listen to any more of your skepticism and hypocritical nonsense! I will figure this out on my own if I have to. I just want to go home."

"A good scientist always approaches results with skepticism," Jazz finally spoke. Her voice calm and non-accusing. "Your days here are numbered and we have no real idea as to how many we have left. It is our hope that Alexa treads your world swiftly to find the answers we need. Your role is to blend in and not get caught."

"By the hunters," Gwen added.

"That is correct," Pico added, "that's my specialty—hunters."

"How do you know so much about them?" Gwen asked skeptically.

"I have always been fascinated by them. They are undetectable—completely invisible."

"Is that right? *I* saw one," Gwen countered the theory.

They gasped—all except for Cat.

"So, I guess you don't know as much as you thought. I hope the rest of your facts are accurate," Gwen's said, her tone acidic. She felt a little thrilled by the opportunity to turn scrutiny on the group.

"You are a special case. You are synthetic," Pico argued.

"Are you sure that's why I can see them? Is that why Alexa suspected I would see the hunters, when others didn't? Did you argue this theory with her before she embarked on her journey?"

"You can't know that," Pico defended.

"Oh but I do. Cat let that one out of the bag." Gwen raised an eyebrow as she spoke.

"I never told you about the argument," Cat finally spoke up in Pico's defense.

"Common sense, and your accusations led me to that rocket-science proving theorem," Gwen said sarcastically. "It's no wonder Alexa lives her life buried in books and her own mind. You friends of hers, are no better than the people of my world. I thought your world was perfect when I woke in it but after meeting you, I'm truely disappointed. Actually, I'm relieved to know that when I return to my world, I won't be missing much." Gwen regretted saying that aloud after her mind flashed Rook's face causing her center to ache and throb. "I'm sorry. I need a minute," Gwen said before placing her face in her hands to massage her head at the hairline.

"Tell me about the hunters," Gwen said—exhausted from defending Alexa.

"Hunters are from the *world of the unseen*—WOTU. They are only known to be seen by *the all seeing*—TAS— whom where born with the gift to know all that is in one's memories. They sift the memories of this world to detect those barbaric in nature: consumption of water, plants, and even animals, killing of other living creatures and people. They are violent to the core. Our people, a jury of our peers, trust in TAS to seek out such individuals, communicate with the WOTU and send hunters out for them."

"What happens once they are caught?" Gwen remembered Cat mentioning execution.

"TAS proves beyond a shadow of a doubt the person is indeed a wardlow—corrupt in mind and spirit—and once in agreement with the jury, they are executed."

"That's crazy! Why are they executed? What if they change back?" Gwen asked astounded.

"They don't change back. According to the legends, a wardlow is nothing more than a parasite that feeds on the soul of a human—corrupting the mind, body and spirit. Execution assures us they will not reproduce and spread like a plague."

"But that's the problem isn't it? It's happening now, more than ever?" Gwen guessed.

"You do have great instincts," Jazz complimented, "You may prove more useful than previously thought."

"Gee, thanks," Gwen said sarcastically.

The group allowed Gwen to soak in the story for a moment and draw whatever conclusions she could. "So, you don't believe a wardlow is beyond repair? You think it's a treatable condition? I mean, if I were caught and executed, in Alexa-form, she couldn't return. What then?"

"We don't know and we *don't* want to find out," Jazz said.

"If you're caught they will see what has taken place today. They will know what we know, and they will come for us all. Finding us will be easier than finding a wardlow —effortless. We wouldn't stand a chance!" Hui-ming said.

Gwen began to understand the importance of Alexa's mission. She wanted to help. *It isn't right—what they are doing to their own people.* For the first time in her life Gwen had the opportunity to do something epic. Unfortunately, she could tell no one. "So, what can I do to help? There must be something aside from blending in?" Gwen said. "What do we do next? Weekly meetings? What?" Gwen asked.

Brendon tapped the tip of his pen against the pad of paper in front of him nervously.

"You think there will be more?" Gwen asked, "Hunters I mean."

"Once they realize your eluding tactics are more than coincidence, we suspect they will get clever. The less people you interact with, the better," Pico warned.

"We will code in on our phones. First digit—time, second digit—number of days, third digit—importance of meeting," Cat said, "So if you receive a 157 message, that means: 1:00, in 5 days, relevance 7 out of 9. That code doesn't really make sense, it's just an example. If something is a 7 out of 9, it most likely won't occur 5 days later. It will be a 0 or a 1."

"So a 909 for instance? Means 9:00, today, emergency?" Gwen asked.

"You are good," Cat replied.

Rook's day dragged on and on. He went to work as his old self—neutral and robotic. Gus, was in a good mood—whistling along to a tune playing in his head. He did a double-take when he noticed Rook's vacant eyes. "What do you know, bro?"

Rook raised an eyebrow but kept his eyes on his work. "You were right—as always."

"'bout what?"

"She doesn't want to see me anymore. Tried to convince me yesterday that we weren't good together." Rook turned his eyes to meet Gus. "She thinks it's best for me. It doesn't make sense. We are completely happy together. Ridiculously happy! I just don't get it!"

"Perhaps she knows something you don't," Gus offered.

Rook looked at him as if that were obvious. "She won't tell me what it is. She thinks she can scare me away or repulse me—ridiculous!"

"Do you trust her judgment? Do you love her enough to trust her?" Gus asked.

"Of course," Rook defended.

"Then you might want to consider that what she says is the truth. What if she is terminally ill? Maybe she doesn't want to burden you or destine you for more loss."

"Man! I didn't think of that." Rook's defenses dropped as he considered the possibility.

"I don't know what it was that caused her to collapse that day. I was so hard-headed yesterday! All I did was stress her out more. I have to apologize. I have to let her know that I care for her enough to set her free." Rook was

119

overwhelmed with guilt and self-pity over the soon-to-be probable loss of his one true love.

"It's not too late. The sooner you stop seeing each other, the easier the separation will be. If she is terminal, her love for you will just prolong your agony—she will inevitably fight to stay here for you—prolonging her own suffering."

"That has to be it. I already can't imagine my life without her. I let my mind wander too far ahead of me. It's my own fault for getting so attached. I should know better."

"I have a surprise for you," Gus said hoping to distract Rook from his sorrow.

The word *surprise* made Rook think about the argument with Gwen the day prior. "Will it cheer me up?"

"I think he's pretty cool." Gus motioned Rook to follow him to the break room.

"He?" Rook asked as he followed dumbfounded.

In the room stood a large cage with a gray parrot inside. A gray parrot with a bright red tail.

"It's an African Gray!" Gus said.

"I see." Rook approached the cage slowly. "Where did he come from?"

"One of our new customers, raises and rescues them. He was so happy with our work that he wanted to thank us by offering us this guy. He says this bird is really smart, friendly, and a boat-load of laughs. I thought of you."

"I have plenty of room for him in the house. What is his name?" Rook asked pleasantly surprised.

"The guy didn't say. Guess he doesn't have one bro."

The bird stood on his perch, feathers fluffed out, one foot curled to his chest.

"Why is he just standing there? Is he sick?" Rook asked.

"The guy said it would take a few weeks or so to warm up to you. He looks relaxed to me. I'm no expert on birds though. I don't think he would give you a sick bird. That would be pretty cruel bro." Gus clasped his hand on Rook's shoulder.

The bird suddenly chimed in with the ring of the shop phone followed by, "Yah-llow?

They laughed together in stereo. "He's pretty sweet!" Rook laughed.

The phone rang in the lobby and in the shop. "I'll get it. Spend some time with your new pal." Gus chuckled as he left the break-room.

Rook approached the cage and saw his new buddy climbing slowly across the bars. "You're pretty smart eh?" The bird hung on the side of the cage—top of his beak clung onto a horizontal bar as he eyed his new companion.

"It's for you, bro," Gus told Rook.

Rook grabbed the phone in the lobby.

"Hello?" Gwen's voice asked.

"I thought you didn't want to see me anymore," he answered defensively.

"I said I shouldn't but I can't stand being away from you," Gwen argued.

Rook thought about what Gus said and changed his tone, "I miss you. And I wanted to apologize for my behavior yesterday. I should have been more open-minded and understanding. I just want you to know that I will honor your wishes either way. I will leave you alone if that's what you want," Rook explained.

The other end of the line was silent.

"You still there?" Rook asked.

"Yeah. I am. I don't know why this is so hard!" A moment of silence again. "You promised you wouldn't blame me later right?" Gwen begged.

"Right," Rook assured her.

Silence again followed by Gwen's quiet words, "Damn me for bringing you into this mess. I need you—like my life depends on it. I don't understand it!" Gwen sighed hard.

Rook closed his eyes as he realized she did share the same feelings—unfortunate—but a relief none-the-less. "I don't think these feelings are reversible. The damage is already done," Rook explained.

"Is that possible?" Gwen asked astounded.

"Totally. We are meant to be together. I don't even know if we have a choice anymore," Rook explained.

"That's not possible," Gwen protested.

"You say that a lot."

"Keep hanging around me and you will understand why." Gwen sighed.

"Is that your final decision?"

Silence on the other end of the line.

"Think about it before you answer, once you have given it, there is no turning back. Unless of course you say no. I will gladly accept a yes later on," Rook said chuckling.

Gwen was afraid he could see her smile over the phone so she tried to contain it.

"Fine. But you have been forewarned. Don't hold me accountable when the pieces start to come together and you decide you don't like the picture revealed."

Rook desperately wanted to change the subject. "You want to go to the State Fair today?" he asked excitedly.

Gwen welcomed the change. "Sure. My phone is on. Let me know when you are on your way. I will try to have your surprise ready when you get here," Gwen said—accepting defeat.

"I'll see you in a little bit."

Rook hung up the phone with a smile and a sense of relief. He went into the break-room to talk to Gus. "I guess it isn't over yet."

"You're asking for it," Gus warned.

"I realize it, but I have to try. I won't be able to live with myself—wondering what could have been. We are bound."

"Coupled?" Gus asked shocked.

"No! We have only been alone together a few times and neither of those times would have been appropriate."

"Don't do it bro! Don't even think about it," Gus pleaded, "you will regret it, I can promise you that much."

"There is a time for everything, and I don't think we are in that stage of our relationship yet."

"I beg to differ. Not to be nosy, but I overheard part of your conversation and I sense trouble on the horizon. You don't know what you're getting yourself into."

"You're right about that. And I'm okay with that. There are only a few certainties in life—very few—death being the most certain of all. Before that day comes for me, I want to have experienced life to its fullest potential. No regrets! Or at least, the right regrets. I am in love with her —orbondwahr! If I die next week, I will rest easier knowing that I did everything in my power to be there for her and enjoy her while having the chance."

Gus sighed hard, knowing he wouldn't win this argument. "This is not going to end well bro. I don't know what is going to happen, but I know it isn't going to be good."

"You do have great instincts bro, just go with me on this one." Rook patted Gus on the back.

Gus shook his head in defeat. "You want help taking the bird home?"

Rook was glad to change the subject. "Sure."

Chapter Twelve

They rode a few rides, and played a few games. Rook was good at all of them, which didn't surprise Gwen. She figured his insight to mechanics played a significant role. He won a giant penguin for her, which she planned to put by her bedside.

Gwen's periphery caught a glimpse of a familiar color, which instantly made her heart race. Instinctively, she whirled around in a complete 360 and saw the khaki-man. *Oh no!* she thought crouched down behind a small coaster ride. Rook panicked but Gwen didn't care.

Rook whispered loudly, "What are you doing?"

Gwen shushed him with a finger and waved him to turn around with her other hand. Completely dumbfounded by what Gwen was doing, he trusted her enough to listen. He immediately looked away and pretended to be looking for someone or something.

Gwen stood once the sense of urgency diminished to a tolerable level. "We've got to go. Right now!" Gwen whispered loudly. She turned and ran through the park hoping Rook was right behind her. Not worried how she would explain the situation she ran on pure instinct. *I will not allow my instincts to be diluted by useless thoughts of what-ifs.*

Gwen heard more than one set of footsteps following behind her. She desperately hoped one set belonged to Rook. *I think the exit is just ahead,* she thought as she swiftly navigated in between various park rides, game stands, and vehicles. Someone grabbed her from behind by the right arm. She squealed knowing the touch was not Rook's. Suddenly overcome by a familiar sense of superiority—in spirit she became the large jungle cat. Instinctively, she spun around counterclockwise toward the hunter, swooping her left arm over-top of his, then snaked her arm underneath to lock out his elbow. She used her leg to swoop his legs out from under the hunter—slamming him onto the ground. Her instincts flowed like water. Her new reflexes were astounding.

The hunter sprung back onto his feet and grabbed the chest of Gwen's shirt to pull her in closer. Gwen chopped the hunters wrist downward, spun it clockwise, locking his elbow out. While behind the bent over hunter, she threw a kick at his rear end knocking him headfirst into a cardboard billboard advertisement.

Rook watched in awe while Gwen fought the invisible force. He grabbed her wrist, "Come on, we've got to hurry, before you draw too much attention to yourself."

Gwen ran with Rook to the fullest of Alexa's physical capabilities.

Rook was right behind Gwen as she ran. *Should I follow her?* He had no time to think it through. His instincts, protective nature, or growing fondness for Gwen, led him to follow her wherever she ran. He was surprised by how well she navigated the fairgrounds. *What was she doing back there? Fighting? Whatever it was I think it's following us, I swear I hear footsteps behind me.* His adrenaline pumped as he heard the footsteps gaining speed behind them. Though he had no idea who was after them or why, he decided that it was beside the point—he didn't want to get caught.

Rook looked closely at the rides, machinery, and vehicles ahead. *I need something big, something nearby—something mechanical.* He hoped his adrenaline would give him the strength to do what he thought necessary.

The fairground exit was now in site. He knew the opportunity to escape, on foot, was growing slimmer by the second. Just as he began to lose hope, he saw what he was looking for, an out-of-order park ride and parked right next to it, what Rook assumed to be a functioning fairground park vehicle. Unsure if he could make the change fast enough Rook grabbed Gwen's arm and pulled her off-course. Her body become heavy. *Perhaps I should have warned her first.* He picked her up effortlessly. *Wow! This fight-or-flight stuff is no joke!* Rook thought as he progressed on his current course without missing a step.

The invisible force chasing them hadn't missed a step. *The footsteps gained speed.* Rook pushed his pace to the max. He was carrying more weight now and feared this could work against him. He hoped all this running wouldn't deplete his abilities effectiveness.

Now is not the time for doubt dummy, you will do this! He heard the footsteps falling behind and this gave him the confidence boost he needed.

Rook winced as he lifted Gwen higher, literally tossing her into the ride's empty seat. The landing looked a little rough. He put his right hand on the nose of the ride, and his left hand on the hood of the parked vehicle. He closed his eyes with complete confidence while combining the two massive items into an aircraft. "I hope this thing has enough power to fly!"

The park ride had an elliptical wheel on a tilt with small orange airplanes attached to it. The larger mass of the park vehicle allowed Rook to increase the mass of the airplane—it's the engine in the vehicle he worried about. *I hope it will be strong and fast enough. This will either work or it won't.*

Rook hopped into the pilot side of the plane, placed his right hand on the black control panel he manifested for himself. The plane gained altitude smoothly. The higher it rose, the more relaxed he felt. Rook wanted to look at Gwen laying in the passenger side but didn't want to become distracted as he flew them to safety.

Gwen woke disoriented. It took a minute for her mind to assemble the images she saw. *I'm on Rook's couch. How did I get here?*

Rook sat across the room in a sofa chair waiting for her to regain consciousness.

"What were we just running from? Are you in some kind of trouble? Do you even remember?" Rook asked questions as quickly as they formed in his head.

"It's complicated." Gwen said as she looked down at the floor. "He wasn't chasing you," she clarified.

"Another long story," Rook said frustrated.

The more time Gwen spent with him, the more she painted herself into a corner.

"As I've mentioned before, I am a good listener," Rook said slowing his pace to stand in front of her. "It seems you have a lot of long stories to tell. So, why don't we start with this one?" He didn't mean for his words to come out so harsh but he was still rattled from their close encounter with some unseen force.

Gwen decided not to think—just speak, "I went to sleep in my world and woke in yours. In a different body, as a different person."

He kept his eyes locked on hers, a perplexed expression washed over his face as her words sank in. She felt more confidence with each spoken word, realizing that the conversation was going more smoothly than anticipated. *He hasn't freaked out yet. Then again he is probably too exhausted to freak out.*

"One person one day, another person the next? Two different worlds? You *do* sound nuts." His tone did not change and she knew from her gift of empathy that he meant this only as an observation. She saw no fear, doubt, or suspicion in his eyes. "You were serious about the different world thing. So what? You visited one of the worlds and ticked someone off and now they are after you?"

"Not exactly. Do you have something I can sketch on?"

"Yeah. In the drawer next to the couch," Rook said remaining calm.

Gwen continued delivering her secret in bite size pieces, as she sketched a picture of the khaki-man. This allowed his mind to fully chew each piece before moving on. "I'm saying that in my world, I have brown hair, green eyes, I am a little shorter and my name is Gwyneth Penn. But when I woke up, the same day I met you, I found all that had changed. My name in this world is Alexa Larissa Murdock. I found out later on, while snooping around her house. A house almost exactly the same as my grandparent's house. If I had known before we met I would have introduced myself as Alexa. She paused to give him time to let it all sink in and to gauge his expression in the mean time.

He was speechless, which made Gwen nervous. She couldn't feel the connection with his eyes when he was deep in thought this way. He was no longer looking at her, he was looking through her.

"Do you see why I didn't want to say anything?" Gwen's eyebrows pulled back with worry.

His face tensed and suddenly he looked angry. "You said that if you had known, you would have introduced yourself as Alexa. You would have lied?" Of all the questions in his mind, for some reason, this was the first one to make it past his lips.

"I'd be lying either way! It's not something you tell someone the first day you meet, and I am pretty sure there aren't rules on how to handle this situation. I have never, literally, walked in someone else's shoes before, but I wonder if the person who developed the expression *did.*"

"You may look like Alexa but you are Gwen," Rook insisted.

"So, do you believe me? Or do you think I'm crazy?" Gwen pressed for an answer. "Here is a sketch of the man who has been after me."

"Seriously? That's just insane. I mean—you can't be..."

"Can't be what? Do you know this man?" Gwen asked anxiously.

"He is no man. You should not even be able to see him! You should not be able to escape him," Rook said amazed.

"Well, this makes two out of two now," Gwen said.

"This is bad. Very bad." Rook looked shocked and anxious.

"What else do you know about the man-thing chasing you?"

Gwen told Rook the story about the day he surprised her and found himself lying on the ground before he could blink.

"He is a hunter." Rook's expression didn't change as he spoke. Rook wanted to believe there was another explanation but in his heart he knew better. He couldn't help but worry what would happen if he got caught protecting her.

"Only you can see him? How did you know to evade him? Wardlows aren't supposed to know they are being pursued. I'm no expert, but I do specifically remember that part of the legend. The Wardlow and the Hunter—nothing but old legend; a myth, so I thought."

"So you ran with me even though you didn't know what you were running from?" Gwen asked shocked. She thought he may have seen him too.

"Yeah. Strange right? I wasn't sure why I was running. I just knew we had to get away. Maybe it's that empathy trick of yours." Rook gave her like punch on the shoulder and smiled. This was the first time his expression changed since learning the truth.

"What should I do? What can I do?" Gwen pleaded.

"Well, one thing is for sure, you can't go back to the house."

Gwen worried and it showed.

"You can stay with me. My house is way too big for just me anyways," he offered kindly.

"Are you kidding me? They will come here!" she protested and then thought better of it—arguing with Rook was pointless. "I am so sorry for bringing you into this mess. I tried to tell you."

"Yes. You did," he said sympathetically, "Wow. A wardlow. You are not at all what I would have envisioned."

"Tell me everything you know," Gwen said solemnly.

Gwen felt a sense of relief, finally able to let it all out. "In my world, people and animals eat and drink to survive. We are not as strong, fast, or athletic. Each of us has something to be self-conscious about."

"Self-conscious? What do you mean by that?" he asked.

"Me for instance. I am a little overweight and my feet are larger than the average female. It makes me feel ashamed."

"But I thought you said everyone has something to feel ashamed of. That doesn't make sense."

"We all have something that we find, in ourselves, to be physically flawed. Some of us have crooked teeth which can be corrected with braces. Big noses can be surgically modified. Some men have balding hair which they purchase rugs to cover."

"What? Like carpet hats?"

She laughed at how serious he was when he asked. *I guess I should choose my words more wisely.*

"Not *carpet.*" Gwen laughed aloud. *"Wigs.* Or there is a surgical procedure where they pull hair from other parts of their scalp, to implant into the balding areas. Doctors make a lot of money on peoples' bad self-image."

"Money?"

"Yes. We survive by means of money."

"I can't believe it!" He sat back up with his feet on the ground. "You live among the barbaric? That's impossible!"

Rook stood up quickly and walked to the picture window where he stared out into *his* world trying to imagine *Gwen's.* "You're *so* not barbaric. You are not like them!" He was so angry, Gwen saw his color change. She never imagined Rook capable of such an intense, hard emotion. "Wardlows are supposedly ruthless, heartless, parasites!"

"I am one of them. I may not be the heartless parasitic kind. I have a job, which I am not crazy about, I have to pay to attend school and I could not survive without money—not in my world. I would be without shelter and without food."

Her heart pounded as he spoke. *He is disgusted by my world and therefore disgusted by me—just as I suspected he would be.*

"You are a slave in your world!" Rook said appalled.

Gwen rose from the couch and made her way to his side. She put her hand on his shoulder. He brought his hand up and set it on top of hers. The warmth and closeness soothed her, returning her heart to a more stable, regular beating pattern. She wrapped her arms around him hugging him tightly. He put one hand on her back and the other on the side of her head, pressing Gwen's face into his chest. *This is where I want to be. Nothing else matters anymore. To return home without him would be worse than death itself.* Her eyes got hot, as if to begin crying, so she pulled herself away from him.

He let her free from his grip and said, "Where are you going? What's the matter?" He looked as though he felt pain from the broken embrace.

Gwen felt the pain in her center too, but a part of her knew it was for the best. I can't let this go on any longer!

"I can't allow myself to feel this way anymore." To say the words aloud hurt internally. She felt as though her bare, vulnerable soul was being whipped with a leather strap. The pain was self-inflicted. *It has to be less excruciating than the pain that awaits me, if I allowed this to go any further,* she reasoned with herself.

"What are you saying? I thought we were past this!" Rook said angered.

"That was before we were, only, footsteps in front of the hunter. Don't you understand—the time will come when I have to leave this world, and go back to my own? I need to be strong for my grandparents. They need me. I owe them my life for what they have sacrificed for me!"

"You can't leave. I think these feelings are irreversible! I would rather die a million times by the worst ways known to man, than lose you!"

Gwen was amazed that either of them held their feelings back for as long as they did.

"You will have Alexa," Gwen said gravely. For her to

return home to such a life made her jealous. Gwen wanted the best of both worlds.

Rook sounded outraged by her suggestion, "It's not the same! It's the soul by which we are connected—not the body—you have to know that much."

"I know. I know. But there is nothing I can do to change it. When the time comes, I have to go! This is going to get very complicated. There is no way to win—checkmate."

"It may never happen," he sounded hopeful. "We should live for now while it still exists for us." He sounded like a stubborn child unwilling to give up the battle.

"You think my leaving would kill us now? What will it do to us if we allow this to continue?" Gwen tried to reason with him.

"It can't get any worse!" he argued.

"Things can *always* be worse," Gwen argued.

"What would be worse is if we torture ourselves now while we still have the chance to enjoy our time together. Please don't deprive me of this, so that your life will be easier. I know you are not that selfish!"

Gwen plopped down on the couch feeling defeated.

"I don't know what to do. I can't stand to lose anyone again. But that is inevitable now isn't it?" she asked in defeat. "I will either go back to my world and lose you or I will stay in this world and lose my grandparents and let's not forget about why I'm here in the first place. I shouldn't have allowed myself to feel this way. What was I thinking?"

"I don't think you had a choice how to feel about me. I don't think any of us really has a choice how we feel about anybody."

He sat down next to her and put his hand on her knee. "Let things be. Things have a way of working themselves out. I sincerely believe that everything has a purpose. Our meeting could not be by chance. Who knows how many times Alexa walked passed my shop on a regular basis.

Neither of us aware of the others existence. Yet the very day that you were brought here, we met and instantly formed this unbreakable connection. I'm not one to question the creator's plan and I would never suggest the work is flawed."

The first time she heard anyone speak of a higher power in this world. Gwen didn't see any churches, just as there had been no restaurants, bars, or banks.

"You believe in God—a creator?"

He looked at her like she was out of her mind. "Of course I believe in the creator! It's not a belief, it's a certainty. Why would you assume otherwise? Does your world question the existence of the creator?"

"Some do."

"That's unfathomable. How could anyone question this?"

"Well, there was a time when people were sure the earth was flat," Gwen said lightheartedly.

This lightened the mood as she intended. He chuckled at the thought and shook his head. "I suppose."

"And in my world, there are probably people who think *that* is a conspiracy, even though it has been proven," Gwen added. "Why aren't there any churches?"

With a confused look on his face, he waited for her to continue.

"You know, buildings where people worship together—congregate? The preacher reads the bible and preaches the words of the Lord."

"I don't understand. Why would we do that? Everyone knows and understands who the creator is. We don't need anyone to tell us. We don't need to sit around and talk about it. We are born with this knowledge."

"You mean, everyone has the same belief system?" Gwen asked amazed.

"Of course!" Rook thought these questions were crazy. He even wondered if Gwen was joking.

Religion is not a conversation Gwen would typically engage in, but this fascinated her. Hard to imagine such a world where everyone agreed on religion, performed jobs that they chose out of passion and were good for the sake of being good.

"About us..." As much as she didn't want to discuss the painfully inevitable future they faced she knew it had to be discussed. "I don't want to be away from you. I don't even know if it's possible." She sighed deeply. "It would be like denying myself the right to breath. Pain followed by death."

"Glad to hear the feeling is mutual," he smiled.

"I wish I could take you to my world and show you it isn't all bad." Just as soon as she said it, a thought barged to the front of her mind. "You want to try something?"

"Sure. Why not?" Rook consented.

"I call it *inducing the calm*. I've been practicing. I wonder if I can take you with me. Last time we did this together, I think my panic messed us up."

"So what do we have to do?" Rook asked.

"Same thing we did at the Dresden sanctuary. Only this time, we both have to remain calm regardless of where our minds take us. We have to focus on each other rather than ourselves. This way, we will stay together. If you are thinking about anything else it will not work and we will get separated."

"Wow. How do you know all this?" Rook asked astounded.

"I don't. You can't be afraid once the calm begins. Oh— just a caution—movement is backward, we need to stay focused and communicate well. Our communication will be telepathic. I suspect our minds will be connected in a way which we will have no secrets. I'm not sure about that part but I wanted to warn you, just in case. I don't want you to think I intentionally high-jacked your mind. You will know mine as well."

Chapter Thirteen

They sat cross-legged facing each other in Rook's living room. Gwen was pleased with how calm and willing Rook was about the experiment. She tried not to get overly excited. *Who knows where we will go if I mess this up.*

Suddenly, they were no longer sitting in Rook's living room. They were standing in Gwen's living room. Gwen kept hold of one of Rook's hands to guide him along. "You see what I mean? Everything is backwards."

Rook's thoughts were everywhere. "Once your mind calms down, you will be able to communicate with me. Right now, all I can hear is your chaotic cluster of thoughts." Gwen smiled. Rook returned the smile.

This was the first time Gwen saw anyone else out-of-body while inducing the calm. Rook appeared almost formless but still recognizable. She reminded herself that he can hear her thoughts too. Rook smiled again.

"This is my living room. As you can see it is similar to that of Alexa's. Gwen focused on her bedroom. They were there in the blink of an eye. "This is me, sleeping." Rook stared at the girl Gwen claimed to be. "Hey. Don't forget I can hear what you're thinking," Gwen reminded him. "Don't hate on the pajamas." Gwen was thankful that she wore pajamas. Rook chuckled in their mind.

"Hey, your cat! Rook shouted in their mind.

"Weird right?" Gwen commented.

"Speaking of weird, I want to show you something you've never seen before." Gwen thought about the flat part of the Penn's roof.

Rook was in awe at his surroundings. They were dark but not too dark.

"A full moon." *Perfect timing,* Gwen thought.

"This is the moon?" Rook asked excited. "Why is it so dark?"

"In my world, it is dark by moon and light by sun."

"What does the sun look like?"

"It's too bright to look at. It will burn your eyes and blind you permanently."

"What are those bright spots and dark patches?"

"The spots are stars and planets. The patches are clouds."

"This is so unreal!" Rook could hardly contain his excitement.

"Maybe for you."

"You should see the colors in the sky when the sun is on the horizon. Layers of color—yellow, orange and red. The trees change color in autumn."

"What's autumn?"

"It's a colder season. It is actually autumn now. If it were daylight you could see for yourself. The leaves change color and fall from the trees. They don't bloom again until spring—another season."

"While I'm here I want to check on my grandparents." Gwen hoped they weren't doing anything she would rather not see.

She thought about Bev and was suddenly disoriented by the change of scenery. Bev was sleeping in a chair against a wall, not the living room chair, but a hospital chair. Gwen began to panic as she turned around to the bed behind her. Her heart told her she already knew who was there. "Grandpa! No!" The terror repelled them back from her world. She tried to hold on and fight against it. "No. Wait!" Everything slipped away from them and they were back to Rook's living room.

Gwen wanted to jump up off the floor and pace but her body was still in sleep paralysis. She felt as if she were sinking in the puddle of mud from her nightmare.

As soon as Gwen was unfrozen she stood up and began pacing the room.

"What happened back there? We were hanging in there pretty good and then bam! We were zapped back here before I knew what happened," Rook said disoriented.

"My grandfather is in the hospital! It's all my fault! I knew this would happen."

"Knew what would happen?"

"I knew something bad would happen the minute I was away from them."

"Maybe it wasn't bad," Rook reasoned.

Gwen glared at him, "The hospital is never good."

"He was alive wasn't he?"

"I think so. I wasn't able to see him. We were zipped back just as soon as I caught a periphery glimpse."

"Don't panic yet. We can just go back there." Rook reconsidered, "Or you could just go back there and get a better look at what is going on."

"I can't induce the calm while in this state of mind," Gwen said frustrated as if it were common sense.

"The best thing you could do for yourself, and your family, is not panic. This is not your fault. You didn't choose to wake up here right?"

"No. I didn't. I have to get back there. If he dies, my grandmother will be alone."

"Technically not," Rook stated.

"It isn't Alexa's problem. She is no more to blame than I."

"What do you know about Alexa? I mean, have you dug into who she is—her past, and present? Who is she? What does she do? What if someone who knows her catches up with you—like the group?"

"I've thought about that. I'm going to do what I did with you. I'm going to say I bumped my head and I have amnesia."

"You are going to have to do better than that if you want to blend in. You *are* a little strange."

"Really? You never seemed to care," Gwen said offended.

"No. I was intrigued by it," Rook explained.

"And now you are just repulsed by it," Gwen defended.

Rook put a hand on her shoulder and his tone turned serious, "No. My feelings for you have not changed. And no matter how much you wish they would, they won't so you can stop wasting your energy on that thought."

"Yeah but now I'm a burden on your life. I have hunters chasing me for who knows what purpose."

"I believe they intend to execute you," Rook explained.

"Gee, is that all?" Gwen asked sarcastically.

"Do you really want to get yourself involved?"

"I don't have a choice anymore. I can't let you do this alone."

Gwen was done arguing with Rook. "The way I see it, if there is a way home, there must be a way back." She didn't want to get either of their hopes up but it felt as if hope was all they had left. Time was slipping away with every breath.

Rook shared his idea, "I think we should go back to Alexa's and look for clues. I don't know what to look for but it just seems like the more you know, the better prepared you will be. You don't even know what all of her abilities are. Empathy can't be your only gift."

"Well, I do have the ability to visit your world and mine when I induce the calm." Gwen added forgetting to mention the animal sight which she had yet to experience. *Maybe Alexa lied to Cat.*

"Plus that other scary place you described the first time," Rook added.

"Yeah. I don't know how I ended up there and I'd rather not return. I still see that place in my dreams. Nothing like that horrifying nightmare I told you about but still, it's so dreary and empty feeling.

"I never put much thought into the whole wardlow thing, but I can tell you this, you are nothing like what I envisioned a wardlow to be."

"So you've said. What do you know of wardlows anyway?" Gwen asked.

"When a person is afflicted with the wardlow, their soul becomes corrupt and corroded to the point of non-existence."

"Like some kind of disease?" Gwen asked dismayed by the description.

"I guess."

"Pure fiction. I have not corrupted her soul. We just simply switched places. What do you think happens to Alexa if they execute me? Why does this even happen? How can it happen? I believe everything happens for a reason. So what is the purpose of such an occurrence?" Gwen brainstormed.

"Some things just aren't meant to be understood," Rook suggested.

"Who's idea is it to execute them? Why take such extreme measures? I am not dangerous?"

"People fear what they don't understand. I assume it's the same way in your world."

"That's my point. This is exactly how things work in my world. Your world is so much better than mine. You are advanced in so many ways. This practice seems barbaric."

"So why is it I am not supposed to be able to see the hunters?"

"I don't know," Rook said shaking his head in a daze.

"I was only here a matter of days when that hunter came for me. He knew where I was. How?"

TAS—the all seeing. They are the ones sending the hunters for you. They monitor the minds of our people for suspicious memories. They literally see everything. Hunters are from the WOTU—world of the unseen but TAS can see them.

"Maybe I'm TAS. I can see them."

"Can you see my memories?"

"No."

"Then you are not TAS. That would be a pretty cool twist though if you were a TAS wardlow." Rook chuckled in amusement.

"You are different though because you *can* see them."

"I don't just see them. I can sense their presence."

"Interesting. Maybe the legend excludes this possibility to keep from frightening people."

"Or they don't know."

"Maybe you're not a wardlow. Maybe you are something else."

"Something that hunters hunt besides wardlows?"

"Who knows?" Rook shrugged.

Aware that she is a synthetic, chemically induced wardlow, she wasn't sure how much she wanted Rook to know. It wasn't Alexa's plan to bring him in. Her group would be horrified if they knew she told an outsider.

"Your gift!" Gwen saw it leaning against the wall unopened.

"It's been such a crazy day that I forgot all about it,"

Rook said.

"Yeah. It's not every day that you get to outrun a hunter," Gwen agreed. The lack of anxiety she experienced surprised her.

"No kidding right? I doubt that has ever been done. I knew you were special," Rook said.

"He pulled the fabric cover off of the painting and observed the black and purple swirls. At first he thought it was a large purple flower, which reminded him of Gwen. Then he blinked a few times and the image transformed into a large black bird with a tear rolling off of the feathers. "Brilliant!"

"I call it *Weeping for Raven.*"

"This is so perfect! You don't know how much this means to me."

He embraced her again, the way she had embraced him earlier.

The urge to be near him never felt as strong as it did in that moment. She felt as if her life depended on it—like ice water after two days of trekking the desert. As if she were a battery in desperate need of a charge. She felt a hunger deep within her core that she didn't understand. The pull in her core felt as if it would flip her inside out! Like treading the edge of complete insanity.

These feelings were new to Rook too. Only the natives of his world had the capacity for such feelings. Only one person could make you feel this way. The one and only person he was meant for. Rook always knew it was her, but she had to choose him too. The fates had predestined their union and it was irreversible. A cruel but true fate they could not escape no matter how they tried.

They drew near each other as if gravity from within their centers had drawn them together like magnets of opposite poles. The closer they were, the less they could resist the force. Logically they knew it was wrong to allow this to happen but the closer their proximity, the less logic could surface—it was drown out by a much more dominate force. Something had ignited in them both, and there was no way to turn it off now.

Their physical center united—first their abdomen and chest clung together. Her right cheek locked in against Rook's chest by the same unstoppable force—both of their palms and forearms had too. Everything seemed to happen at once with a bang. Before they had time to see what happened to themselves physically, there was a bright explosion of white light overwhelming their senses. When they *could* focus, they were within each others embrace like lovers of Gwen's world—but *they* were out-of-body.

Their surroundings disappeared—they were alone in a pure white place in space, and time, which existed outside of either of their realities. Both too consumed in the heat of the moment—to notice their surrounding environment— the way it was meant to be. When their physical bodies united, the circuit was complete. The pull Gwen had been experiencing within her center was finally satiated. As if in this out-of-body state, they were one. The flames of their souls burned a brilliant blue and white flame together as one larger flame. No other feeling in the world—Rook's nor Gwen's—would ever come close to the *coupling*.

Once the peak of the flame tamed to blue embers, their surroundings dimmed into the real-life color of their previous environment, where their physical bodies resided, still coupled against one another like leaning up against one's own reflection. With the exception that Rook was taller than Alexa. Their eyes opened slowly and simultaneously, seemingly snow-blind. Their core gravity had retracted back into its place—within their soul centers —freeing them from their inseparable bond. Both souls resonated with the same sensation of inseparability. Though physically free from the coupling bond—the farther away they were from one another—the more hollow they would feel from this moment forward. They would forever crave each others company above all else. They experienced only a fraction of this craving before the coupling but now the feeling would cut deeper—a permanent brand on their souls.

The relaxation made it difficult to stand. She pushed it from her mind and focused on the feeling within her amazing—most likely—temporary body. *"Soak it up while ya can kid,"* her grandmother's voice said in her head.

The coupling had sealed their fate together. Rook knew there was a chance that Gwen would return to her old world someday leaving him to mourn the love of his life. Deep down in his soul, he didn't worry about it. Rook didn't live by the constraints of what-ifs and should-not-haves. He learned the hard way through the trauma of losing most of his family—a life with regret is not a life worth living. He decided he would honor the memories of his mother by living his life to the fullest. He felt guilty about Gwen's ignorance to what just happened. What would happen to her if she did go back to her old body, in her own world? Would she be forever empty for no apparent reason (if she forgot about this world)? Could this have ruined her life and a chance at happiness when she returned. He didn't want to worry about these things right now. This was the happiest day of his life. *Everyone looks forward to the day when they meet their special someone. It's natural to fear losing them. We are mortals after-all and eventually it's going to happen anyway.* In this case Gwen wouldn't be going to a better place to wait for him. *Would we see each other in the afterlife?* Rook pushed these thoughts to the back of his mind for now. *I won't let anything ruin this moment.*

Waking in complete darkness, Rook heard a voice calling his name, just above a loud whisper.

"Rook! Wake up," the voice called persistently.

Rook shook the cobwebs from his sleepy mind, rolled over to the edge of the bed and stuck his head out of the dark veil, which pillared down from the ceiling. Startled, he jumped back, almost screamed and then looked out again. "Raven! What are you doing here? How did you get here?"

"Shh—you'll wake her," Raven said.

"You know about Gwen?" *I must be dreaming,* he thought.

"You're not," Raven responded.

Rook's eyes widened, "You a mind reader now?"

"I know you have a lot of questions but I don't have time to answer them. You need to listen to me. She is trouble! She is using you to keep from getting caught. They will catch you both."

"What! She is not using me! I *want* to keep her safe."

"Is that what you really want? Are you sure? Or is that her own agenda projected onto you? Haven't you ever found yourself arguing with yourself over the right thing to do?"

Rook couldn't deny anything—Raven was reading his every thought.

"Haven't you ever wondered if you were truly arguing with yourself, or if it was another force outside of yourself you were arguing with?"

Rook had never considered the possibility and he

didn't want to believe it now.

"Why are you coming to me now? If you know so much why not come to me sooner?"

Rook didn't want to believe anything she said, but at the same time he wanted to reach out, hug her and never let go. "Why didn't you let me know you were okay?"

"Too many questions. I told you. I can't stay and I don't have time. I'm breaking the rules by talking to you. I was getting desperate and had to do something to try and protect you."

"What am I supposed to do?" Rook asked hopelessly.

"There is always a hunter nearby. You need to lure her out before they find you protecting her. If you turn her in, they will not execute you."

"I can't do that! She is my twin soul!" Rook defended.

"Impossible Rook! She isn't even a person anymore! She has no soul. It's tarnished by the presence of the wardlow. You know that!"

"You can read my mind so you know that I don't believe it. You cannot convince me that she has no soul! I've coupled with her."

"More mind games. She is a parasite. She will feed off of you until there is nothing left. And then she will move on to the next sucker."

Rook put his head in his hands. He wanted this conversation to end and he wished it had never happened.

"I can see that my warning has done no good. Keep your eyes and ears open. I pray that you will do the right thing when the time comes."

"Will I see you again? Will you ever wake?"

"Too many questions. None of them relevant." Raven faded into nothingness.

"Wait! Don't go!" Rook reached out into thin air.

"You disappoint me brother," Raven's voice said fading into silence. Rook's heart sank.

Rook lay back down staring into the darkness. *She tried to push herself away from me before, but I persisted. Could she have been playing me the whole way? It can't be. We couldn't couple without being destined to one-another. Raven said it was a trick. Could something so intense be unreal?* Rook thought about abandoning Gwen, turning her in to the hunters. His stomach churned with ill despair. *I can't do that! I won't do that!*

Rook thought about the disappointment he heard in Raven's voice. *She's trying to look out for me. She said she was breaking rules. Why was she evading my questions? She didn't even mention the songs. She could have at least commented. How do I even know it was her? What if she were the trick?* Rook didn't want to believe that his sister was the phony and Gwen was the real deal. It went against all he had learned in life; family stuck together. Gwen was family too. *What was done cannot be undone. Raven knows that, so why would she wait? If she were so desperate, I could think of better times to intervene than now. I don't know how it works though. I don't know anything about the rules she spoke of. Why not tell me if she'd be back or not?*

Chapter Fourteen

Feels like I'm in heaven, Gwen thought. Waking from the most peaceful sleep of her life. For a moment Gwen thought she may have dreamed the whole thing. When she opened her eyes and saw Rook's loving and perfect face, she sighed. *How could I have been so lucky?* Her mind had not gone to that place of worry and negativity yet. She was so overwhelmed by the whole experience—rejuvenated in a way she never could have imagined. She lay there without movement or thought for a few minutes until one found its way in. *What if I got Alexa pregnant?* Gwen's calm, relaxed, Zen state was now drowned out by sheer panic.

"What's wrong?" Rook sensed her sudden anxiety.

She wasn't sure how things worked in this world as far as love, marriage, and the baby carriage goes. Sheepishly she thought, *how do I ask this question,* "I uh... was just wondering something." She stalled while considering her next words.

"About?" Rook asked just as she imagined he would.

"What happened last night..." She didn't even know what to call it.

Rook sighed. He knew there was no getting around the topic but was hoping she wouldn't start asking questions so soon. He hadn't thought of the easiest way to break it to her. "Does this not happen in your world?" Rook hoped so.

"Not like that! I don't even know what to call that. Holy cow!" Her eyebrows went up.

"Coupling," Rook answered, smiled and almost laughed

at her facial expression as she recalled the event from her perspective. "A totally spiritual experience only shared between twin flame souls. We are spiritually married." He winced as he spoke, hoping she wasn't going to be as upset as she had the right to be.

"Married?" Gwen's tone increased in pitch and decreased in volume as she spoke the word. She thought for a moment. The marriage part was unexpected and almost made her forget her real concern. "I couldn't have... gotten... pregnant or anything right?"

Rook laughed aloud. "Is that what you were worried about?" He sighed with relief at her lack of upset with the marriage part. "No. It doesn't work that way. You have to be able to couple to conceive but physical things have to happen for that to take place and it's a completely conscious decision."

"Really?" Gwen was fascinated by this fact. "So, what you're telling me is, there are no unwanted pregnancies in your world? And not just any two people can make a baby?"

Rook's face was looking back at her like, *Are you seriously asking me this or are you just messing with me?* The perplexed look didn't fade, so he realized she was indeed seriously asking. "That is correct. And in your world?"

"You *don't* want to know. The less you know about my kind, the better."

"You can't be all *that* bad." Rook had no concept of just how different their worlds really were. Gwen's kind were ruthless and barbaric in comparison. Gwen feared that if Rook knew what her people were really like, he could never look at her the same. If he looked at her in disgust, it would just about kill her. The light within her soul would dim until it no longer had the will to burn, and her new body would shrivel into lifeless flesh.

A ring tone came from another room. Gwen wondered

if she had left her phone somewhere then saw it sitting on the nightstand by Rook's bed.

"Yah-low?"

Gwen sat up in a panic. "Someone's here!"

Rook laughed, "No. That's my bird."

"You got a bird?" Gwen asked surprised.

"A customer gave him to me as a gift—he raises them."

"Oh. What's his name?"

"I don't know, I've been just calling him Bird. He seems to respond to that just fine."

"Are you ready to dig through Alexa's stuff?" Rook asked.

"Ready as I'll ever be I guess." Gwen shrugged as she mentally prepared herself for the trip to Alexa's house.

Gwen's phone began to buzz in her pocket. It was a text message—214. She sighed.

"What's the matter?" Rook asked.

"I have a group session at 2:00 tomorrow. If they find out about us, they will be beyond furious."

"They know about you?" Rook asked.

"I'm not supposed to talk about it. It's best if I keep the details to a minimum in case either of us get picked up."

"Do you think the hunters will come for me?"

"Once they figure out that I can see them, they may up the stakes. That is why I didn't want you to get involved."

"If TAS can see all, why haven't they figured it out yet?" Rook asked.

"I don't know, maybe they weren't looking for it. But I bet after yesterday, they have a pretty good idea. And they have to be on to you by now."

Going back to the house was not as nerve wracking as they expected. Somehow they maintained their calm demeanor.

Gwen led Rook to the basement. "I did a little digging down here already, but that was before our chaotic fair experience. Honestly, I didn't have a clue what I was looking for."

"Did anything catch your eye?"

"Just about everything." Gwen's expression changed as a mental light bulb flickered in her mind. She rushed over to the locked desk. "This was locked, but the key wasn't hidden. But these drawers here," she said pointing to the other locked drawers, "I couldn't find the key for them."

Rook smiled confidently as he walked to the locked drawers. He sat in the chair, opened the middle drawer where the writing utensils were, and thoughtfully browsed the items inside. "This will work," Rook said picking up a medium-sized metal clip. Holding the clip in his left hand and placing his right hand over the lock he focused on the contraption required to open the desk.

"You *are* handy," Gwen said amused.

Rook unlocked the drawers and found hundreds of number-coded files. He sat back in the chair and sighed.

"What do those numbers mean?" Gwen panicked.

"It means we are going to be here a while," Rook said sarcastically.

They each took 10 files to start with. Gwen opened the first file anxiously. "What *are* these?" Gwen thumbed through the paperwork and diagrams.

"They look like medical records," Rook said thumbing through the first file.

"You have got to be kidding me!" Gwen's expression changed.

"What?" Rook asked anxiously.

"I could be wrong, but I think these patients are wardlows. Listen to this, symptoms: enhanced color and sound, sensations of vibration, delusional, extreme memory loss."

"It doesn't mean they are wardlows. They could have some other mental condition."

Gwen sighed and persisted, "They are just like me."

Rook took a closer look at the file in *his* hand. The symptoms are basically the same in this case except for a few things; violent behavior, screaming fits, and throwing things. I guess they aren't all like you."

"Hey! That reminds me," Gwen pulled the file she found a few days ago. "Check this out." Gwen handed Rook the paperwork she had already skimmed through:

He was attacked by a patient who lost his mind during a voluntary procedure. The patient was injected with the serum to produce the side-effects mimicking that of the wardlow mind-frame.

His death was a tragic accident and an underestimation of the patient's strength. He kept the details of his research from everyone and led them all to believe that he thought the wardlow was simply a person suffering with a rare mental disorder, which could be cured with the right treatment. It wasn't a complete lie, just a non-updated suspicion. The final belief was so far-fetched that he couldn't bring his colleagues into it. He was afraid they would turn him in.

Rook read the article and dropped the paper with a dazed look on his face. Gwen could almost see the gears turning in his mind.

"These aren't just any old medical records—this is research. This doctor was killed while chemically inducing a wardlow. He injected a test subject to bring about these same symptoms and was killed in the process."

"According to *this* document, the doctor performing the tests was killed about five years ago. He suspected the wardlow was a treatable condition. It also implies that his most recent suspicions were not shared with his staff."

"Can I see that again?" Gwen asked.

"Sure. Do you think it will make more sense if you read it yourself?" Rook joked.

Gwen took the document and skimmed the pages. "Doctor Alexander Murdock!" Gwen slammed the packet on the desk and put her hand to her forehead squeezing the corners of her eyes.

"You alright?" Rook asked with sudden alertness.

Gwen sighed. "This just makes everything more real to me. The doctor was Alexa's father. This is what we came to find down here—sort of. If Alexa wanted me to find it you would think she'd leave a hint or at least a key."

"Alexa's father died five years prior to her becoming a wardlow. Is she doing this just to avenge her father?" Rook wondered aloud.

"I don't want to be here anymore. I don't feel safe," Gwen cringed.

"Let's gather some things to take back to the house. We can research them there."

Gwen took her furry friend out to the car. She kissed him on the top of his head and rubbed his furry little cheeks once they were buckled in and ready to go. Her heart gave a few heavy beats at the sight of his sweet little face. "I missed you."

Rook was astounded by the affection she showed the cat. Just for a moment he wondered if Gwen loved her cat more than him. He knew that was a ridiculous thought but he had never seen such hands-on human interaction with an animal. Gwen paid no mind to Rook as she talked to her little prince charming.

"So, what's the deal with the cat?" Rook asked.

"Whinny is my little prince charming. I've had him since I was a kid."

"That doesn't make sense. Isn't Whinny Alexa's cat?"

"No. Technically, Chester is Alexa's cat," Gwen said. "I know what you're asking but I don't have an answer for you. He looks and acts the same around me as my cat. And I would swear on my life that Chester and Whinny were the same cat, but like most things I've experienced since waking here, it's just not possible."

"Maybe cats are generic when it comes to affection," Rook suggested.

"Oh no. Definitely not. This I know for sure. Cats are finicky, moody little buggers. Chester and Whinny's stripes and spots are exactly the same. Not-to-mention he is cross-eyed. What are the odds? It doesn't make sense but I'm sure it isn't nearly as relevant as everything else going on."

A wave of relief poured over them stepping into the Dresden house.

Rook pulled a green bamboo leaf-covered journal out of a box. The journal had a combination lock holding the pages tightly bound. "I can open this if you want."

"I'm not sure if we should," Gwen warned cautiously.

"Why not? It would be crazy not to open it. We opened the locked drawers." Rook pleaded.

"I'm afraid it will complicate things more," Gwen

whined.

"Do you really think things could get more complicated?"

"I just get the feeling that when I'm supposed to open it, I will know how. Some sort of intuition. Let's keep looking."

Rook threw it on the table between the couches. "Whatever. The curiosity is going to kill me and you know it."

"Then I will just have to find a way to keep your mind occupied." Gwen approached him and put an affectionate hand on his chest, followed by her cheek. Rook put his arms around her and enjoyed the moment. His worries disappeared and all he could think about was her warmth. He wished things could stay so simple and tried not to dwell on what was to come. He would not waste such a moment by stressing about another.

"Mission accomplished," he said quietly.

Gwen pulled away from him slowly, looking him directly in the eyes as she brushed her right hand across his cheek and pushed his hair back a few times—like petting the side of an animal's face. She wanted to show him how her kind showed affection but was afraid of where that could lead. "I don't know how, but I am going to make this work out. No matter what it takes. I will fix this. We will be together." Rook's arm pulled her close to him again. He experienced the magnetic pull, which she attempted to describe to him before. He recognized the feeling as a cocktail of emotion—love with a twist of impending doom. He never experienced the combination until now.

"Let's try not to worry about that right now. Just for now," Rook said quietly. He would hold her like this forever if it were possible.

"I will find a way back to you." Gwen's voice was thin

and weak with the weight of her words.

"What if Alexa doesn't want to stay in your world? Your decisions affect her life too."

"She wasn't so thoughtful when she dragged me into this mess," Gwen defended. "I want to show you how we share affection in my world. Close your eyes and relax."

Teaching him how to kiss was rewarding to Gwen in so many ways. She didn't feel like the awkward teenage girl with no experience—it was just the distraction they needed to take their minds off of their dilemma. All other research was put on the back-burner just for now.

They spread various information across the living room floor and attempted to piece relevant items together.

"Do you understand any of this?" Gwen asked while handing a flipped packet to Rook—the page with the diagrams and equations.

"For the most part. I studied some of these theorems in my mechanics classes. I took physics, chemistry, and even a biology class out of curiosity."

Gwen gave him a wary expression.

"What? I like science," Rook defended.

"Do you like it enough to know what any of this means?"

Rook flipped through the attached pages and back again. "Not exactly. I can tell you that this is chemical and biological, but most of my knowledge is physics-based."

"Can we use it to help understand my condition?"

"I don't see how it would be useful. It's not like you are going to inject some chemical. Right?"

Gwen didn't answer fast enough.

"Right?" Rook insisted.

"Right. It would be pointless," Gwen finally agreed.

"So, we know that I'm a chemically induced wardlow, as part of some experimental research performed by Alexa in honor of her father. I don't understand what she thought was going to happen. Didn't she worry about the hunters coming for me? Why would she take such a chance? She didn't even leave any explanation or instructions for me to follow. What does she expect to find in my world anyway?"

"We still have the journal," Rook reminded her.

"No combination code. You don't think she knew I would meet you or someone else who could open the journal do you?"

"Let's see what else the files tell us," Gwen insisted, then began to read aloud. "Losing her at three, I have no real memory of her. Learning the truth about my father makes me question the truth about my mother. Did she really die in childbirth? Was she involved in wardlow research? Did my father keep his secret from her? When did he start the research and why?"

"This sounds like journal stuff. So, what do you think is in the bamboo journal?" Rook asked.

"You weren't kidding, not opening it is going to drive you crazy." Gwen chuckled at Rook's fixation on the mysterious journal. "Do you see anything pertaining to the hunters? Anything about her own experimentation?"

"I haven't seen the hunters mentioned once."

"This is such a waste of time." Gwen sighed.

"Something is missing. We must have overlooked something." Rook insisted. "It's probably something so small that we missed it."

"Like hiding in plain sight?" Gwen asked skeptically.

"I guess you could say that."

"What do we know? Let's profile her," Gwen suggested.

"She is an artist and a loner, loves her cat..."

"Extremely bold, if she truly did inject this chemical on her own," Rook said.

"Bold or stupid," Gwen suggested.

"Well, think about what this means. We're not looking at the big picture here." Rook's tone was suddenly higher and more excited. "If she was able to induce the swap, than that means wardlows are indeed innocent and should not be executed."

"And just what is my role in all of this? Just don't get caught? There has got to be more to it. Whatever it is, she kept if from her group."

"A non-updated suspicion perhaps?" Rook articulated.

"An accurate one I hope," Gwen said intimidated.

"Hey. I'm going to stop by the hospital. Do you feel alright hanging out here for a while?"

"It's no problem. I want to try and check in on Grandpa —alone would be best. I might take a nap while your are out, I'm still tired."

Rook smiled. "I miss you already."

In this moment Gwen felt that she made the right choice. If she died today, she would die happy. The magnetic pull in her center changed since the bond was formed. She could be near him now without feeling as if she were going out of her mind. The thirst for that connection had been quenched for now.

Chapter Fifteen

Rook decided he needed to see the *real* Raven. He hoped that last night's encounter would bring about something new.

"Mr. Dresden?" An unfamiliar nurse spoke. Rook wondered for a moment how she knew him.

"Rook." He tucked his fist to his chest and said, "Mr. Dresden sounds old." Rook smiled. The nurse smiled and introduced herself, "I'm Seven."

"Seven? Your height says you are a lot older than that," Rook joked. He felt wrong after saying it. He didn't particularly care for some of the responses he had gotten upon introducing himself.

"My parents were expecting a boy whom they would call Evan. I guess they thought Seven sounded more feminine." Rook observed her bubbly upbeat attitude and wondered if it were because she was new. Her charms were lost on him.

"So, how may I help you today Seven?" Rook asked formally.

"Well sir—"

"Rook," he interrupted shifting his weight to his front foot as he corrected the nurse.

"Rook. It seems you forgot to sign one of the documents the other night."

Rook thought for a moment. *What documents?*

Seven didn't have to be a mind reader to know he was confused. She put a finger up and ran back to where the rows of files were kept. She pulled out a thick file, took a packet from the top and handed it to Rook. The nurse set the remainder of the file on the nearby desk.

"Permission to Terminate Life-Support! What is this?" He was astounded and outraged by this unexpected and unfamiliar document.

The nurse bit her bottom lip and didn't speak right away. She waited another moment before speaking again while Rook flipped through each page of the packet skimming the pages.

"This is scheduled for today!" Rook was yelling now.

"Uh—yea—but you forgot to sign the third page. We cannot complete the request unless all pages are signed."

"I didn't sign these! How did this happen? Who would do this to me?" Rook was pulling his hair at the sides and pacing now. "I want these documents destroyed! Immediately! I want to see them destroyed before I leave this hospital!"

"Yes sir! Rook. Follow me."

Rook's mind ran at full capacity. *How could this have happened? Who would know enough about me to pull this off? A nurse? Why? Could it have been a mistake made by the new nurse? My signature was on the paperwork. Identical!* Rook thought about Raven's warning. *Gwen had nothing to do with this!* In his mind Rook heard Raven say, *"you disappoint me brother."*

"Why would she do it?" Rook silently argued with the voice in his head.

"Why do you think? She knows that I'm trying to warn you and she is trying to stop me," the voice argued in Raven's tone.

Rook's silence made Seven uncomfortable as they walked the halls to the room with the massive shred machine.

Seven pushed the door open with her left hand and

leaned in on her elbow. The door opened effortlessly. "This way," she nodded ahead.

"Do you know anything about this?" Rook asked calmly. "I mean do you know who witnessed me sign the documents or who handled them?" Rook continued. "Did anyone sound surprised to hear about it? Everyone here knows me. I wasn't even here the day these documents were supposedly signed."

"I'm sorry Rook. I've only been here for four days and I've been so overwhelmed by all of the new faces and getting familiar with the current cases. I wouldn't have noticed anything out of the ordinary. I am pretty sure that I saw you though. Today was not the first time.

"That's impossible! I haven't been here in the last four days!" Rook shouted and then apologized, "I'm sorry, this is a huge mistake, and I'm not sure how to prevent it from happening again." Rook unintentionally stopped walking. "You said you saw me. Are you sure it was me?"

Seven, sounding a little embarrassed, "I'm sure. I uh— kind of pointed you out to one of the nurses and she told me who you were. That is how I recognized you today." She bit her lip.

Rook did not notice her chagrin. Cute girl, but Rook's heart had been stolen by the allegedly wretched wardlow.

Rook personally shredded the documents, which made him feel a little better. *How can I prevent this from happening again if I don't know how it happened in the first place?*

"*It's her,*" the voice was back.

"*No. That is unacceptable. I won't believe it without proof.*" Rook walked silently alongside Seven meanwhile arguing with the voice in his head.

"*You believe the wardlow over your own sister?*"

"*No. You are not my sister. You are a voice inside my head. I should stop off to get my head scanned while I'm here.*

161

Besides, I can't believe her word over yours—she doesn't know about any of this insanity."

"Probably just another one of those secrets she keeps to herself." The voice was right about Gwen's secrecy. Of course the voice knew how insecure Rook was about Gwen's secrecy—it came from his own head.

Rook visited Raven as usual. Nothing changed since the last time he visited. He sang her songs and told her stories. He didn't mention seeing or hearing her in his head. Seeing Raven's sweet little face was refreshing. The version of Raven from his delusion was rough and tattered in comparison—like a bad impersonation of the sweet, kind-spoken little girl. He put all negative thoughts aside for his visit.

Rook walked in the door and found all was quiet. Then he remembered Gwen said she was planning on inducing the calm while he was gone. He figured she was taking a nap.

Suddenly he heard a knocking noise overhead. *What the heck is she doing up there? Remodeling?*

Rook ran upstairs, pushed open the bedroom door. The thumping noise was louder as he opened the door. Gwen was convulsing on the floor. The back of her head thumped loudly against the solid surface of the floor.

Rook felt fire in his gut—like a heated blade impaling him as he stumbled toward her. He swooped her up into his arms and sat on the bed with her. Her tremors were stiff and short. He positioned her body safely on the bed.

Feeling helpless he gripped her hand in both of his. *What if this is it? What if Alexa opens her eyes instead of*

Gwen? Panic swept his flesh leaving goosebumps behind.

The tremors slowed. Rook rubbed her arm in hopes of soothing whatever discomfort she might be experiencing. He felt heat rising from her body before his fingers touched her face.

"Come back to me Penguin," Rook whispered softly in her ear as he rubbed the side of her face, brushing the hair aside.

The tremors faded to inconsistent twitching episodes.

Rook sat back to assess her. He reached for her hand again.

Her eyes began to flutter the way they had in the Dresden sanctuary. *I'm not going to panic this time,* Rook told himself. *She will be fine, just like before.*

Rook braced himself for her to speak. Her blank, glassy-eyed stare was unsettling. He waited patiently for her to come out of her trance-like state.

Finally, she slowly turned her head to look at him.

"Gwen? Do you know where you are? Is everything alright?" Rook asked calmly.

She blinked slowly a few times before speaking.

"I saw her," Gwen said and then swallowed hard.

Rook felt the fluid of his spine freeze. He straightened his posture as the ice climbed up the back of his neck to the base of his skull. "What do you mean? Who did you see? What did you see? I need to know!" Rook couldn't tell if he were angry, impatient, or what emotion he was feeling.

Gwen pulled away from his grip. "I need a moment to think." Rook looked upset which made her feel unsafe. Gwen apologized in advance, "I didn't mean to invade your privacy. I don't have control over it yet. I wanted to check in on my grandfather but I couldn't. Then I thought of you, and I was automatically taken to you—to the hospital." Gwen felt like crying, but her emotional capacity had not reached full. "You're mad at me." Gwen reached to wrapped her arms around him.

Rook found it impossible to argue with her now. He felt guilty for crushing her delicate emotions, but it didn't stop him from growing suspicious. Could you read my mind too?" Rook hoped she had not.

Gwen pulled her face from his shirt to look him in the eyes. "No. Why? Were you thinking something bad?"

"Since you were spying on me, and now I know you can do so, I guess I'd just like to know how much privacy I'm allowed." The excuse seemed solid to Rook.

"Are you altering my mood?" Rook asked.

The question offended her. "No! Should I?" She pulled away from Rook's side and pouted.

"I didn't mean to offend you. I was just curious," Rook defended.

"It sounds like you don't trust me! I only altered your feelings once and that was an accident. I was feeling sympathetic at the time. Right now I feel... feel... I don't know what I feel! I don't like it. I expected this kind of reaction when you found out I was a wardlow!" Gwen pouted with her arms crossed, eyebrows crumpled as she stared ahead at a blank spot on the wall.

"I do trust you. That's the problem." Rook looked at the floor as he spoke the last part under his breath in defeat.

Gwen shot a ticked off glare in his direction. She was surprised by how upset and betrayed she felt at the moment. She wondered if in the future she should say anything. This was such a shock.

Gwen had no idea what other worries Rook had to deal with. He hadn't been fully honest with her. Knowing this, Rook calmed down and wanted to know more. "So what exactly did you see?" To Rook, his moments with Raven were confidential. Those were the days he spilled his guts about just about everything. He felt confident that he would stick by Gwen's side and not question her guilt, but there was a part of him that was on alert, especially given light of new events. He wanted so much for that shred of doubt to go away. When Gwen was near him, it was difficult to doubt her. When he saw the pain on her face it ripped at his center. He felt guilty for such thoughts.

"I don't want to lie to you about anything. I won't keep any secrets from you anymore. I am insanely in love with you. I mean that with every shred of my being. I've never been more sure of anything in my life. Please don't be upset. I saw too much. I didn't want to invade on your privacy but once you began to play and sing I was spellbound. You are some kind of amazing. Little Raven does look peaceful."

Rook was surprised that this didn't upset him. It felt as though he understood her curiosity and he was flattered by her intrigue of his music. She was family now and did deserve a formal introduction. "Why don't you come with me to the hospital next week?" Rook offered.

"Are you sure?" Gwen was gauging her own feelings about going.

"Yeah. Why not? Maybe you can bring her to life the way you brought me to life."

Gwen blushed. "Oh, stop being so dramatic. You don't have to lay it on so thick. Of course I want to meet her. Don't expect any miracle on my behalf. All I seem to attract is trouble."

"What's that supposed to mean?" Rook gave her a coy look.

"You know what I mean smarty pants!" Gwen lightly slugged Rook in the shoulder.

"Whoa killer, watch it, I don't want you to get any ideas about body slamming me or anything. You got a little mean streak in you don't you?" Rook teased.

"Vile," Gwen agreed with a mock squint-eyed slyness. Rook chuckled. He could not fathom the idea of her as the bad guy. *Inconceivable. Complete nonsense.* He would wager his life on it. *Raven is mistaken. What am I saying? She is in a coma and lately a figment of my imagination. Probably some subconscious way of dealing with my own self-doubt.* For the first time in years, Rook was happier than he ever thought possible and he was not ready to see it end. If Gwen was the bad guy, Rook was sure he'd die a happier man than not having known her.

Rook lay awake within the darkness of his bed with Gwen by his side. He had too much on his mind to let it run recklessly to the dreamworld. He tried to piece things together but found the deed overwhelming. *Why does everything have to be so complicated? Why couldn't I have a normal life? Why did my family have to be torn from me? Gwen will be torn from me one way or the other. I can fight for her though. I will protect her!*

As Rook feared, the voice returned.

"What do you want?" Rook asked in his mind.

"You saw what happened today at the hospital," Raven confronted.

Rook frowned and waited.

"That unsigned document was no accident Rook. It was a warning!" Raven said harshly.

The fire churning in his center was now spiraling outward. *"Who is responsible for this? How? Why would they threaten to kill you? How do they even know about you? Besides, I thought you said it was Gwen's fault. For every* question Rook thought, another surfaced in his mind.

"Too many questions brother. The formless are responsible and fully capable of following through on the threat. If you don't deliver Gwen to the hunters, they will kill me to punish you. While you're guard is down while your mourning me, they will find a way to get her. It's only a matter of time. She hasn't even scratched the surface of her full capabilities. The sooner you turn her in the better. It is her fault."

"If they have that much power and control, why don't they come here and take her from me? Why must I turn her in? Obviously, they know where she is. What gives?" Rook argued with his hallucination.

"She is on the ultraviolet spectrum, the formless cannot manipulate her the way they can the others. She can sense the hunters in ways only a V-spectrum wardlow can. This makes her dangerous and unpredictable. The hunters don't understand how the spectrum works yet. But they are close."

"I don't understand any of this. The formless? Color spectrum wardlows? I thought a wardlow was a wardlow. What do these formless get out of executing wardlows? Am I just a pawn in this game?"

"You are farther in the dark than you may ever know. I should not be talking to you about this. If the formless find out I'm talking to you they will kill me," Raven pleaded.

"I need to know what I'm fighting. Who is running the show? All hunters are formless, but are all formless hunters?" Rook pleaded back.

"You cannot fight and win. Turn her in. I'm begging you, with all of the light remaining in my soul. I will return one day and I don't want to be alone," Raven begged.

"Do you really mean that? You will come back? Why haven't you?"

"I don't have time to explain. Just trust and listen to me. When I come back, we are going to rescue father from that place he's lost himself in. He might as well be one of the

formless wasting away the way he is. His body is useless to him, it's like a stalled vehicle."

"What will they do to her? O'bondwahr (our hearts beat as one), I cannot just abandon her. I will be a shell of a man if they take her away from me," Rook said helplessly.

"They will safely send her back to her own world. That is the evacuation process brother," Raven assured Rook.

"Evacuation? Don't you mean execution?" Rook exclaimed loudly in his mind.

"Her soul will exist in the world in which it belongs. Gwen will no longer live in Alexa's body. She will finally be home with her friends, family and the life that she has been missing for so long now. She cares for you brother, but the truth is, she is very much homesick. You are keeping her from living her life. There are others that depend on her for support. You cannot be so selfish. "

"So, what of Alexa? What comes of her life?"

"Alexa's soul was absolved by Gwen's presence. Gwen's soul will vacate the premise and the formless will dispose of the body."

"What is going on with Gwen's old body? Are you sure it will be there waiting for her return? Are you sure you know what you are talking about? How do you know?"

"I don't know what is happening on the other side. I cannot see into Gwen's world," Raven said sincerely. "I wish I could offer you more comfort in that fact."

Gwen meant what she said about the desire to keep no more secrets from Rook but found herself unable to tell Rook everything. Gwen did see Raven in the hospital but that wasn't the only encounter she had with her.

"We need to talk," Rook said halfheartedly.

"You're right. I have something I need to tell you."

"May I have a walk with that talk?" Gwen tried to sound upbeat to counter his gloomy tone.

"A walk sounds good," Rook agreed.

"You sound alarmed, you're making me nervous," Gwen commented.

"Do you miss home?" Rook asked seriously, "I *know* you do. I guess what I mean to ask, if you could go home today, would you?" Rook didn't look her in the eyes after asking the question.

Gwen began to slouch and drag her feet as they walked. She looked to the ground as if the answer would rise from there. Gwen's chest began to ache with the familiar storm cloud. She hadn't experienced the longing sensation since moving in with Rook and keeping close to him. "I miss my grandparents. I need to know my grandfather is fine. But then, I know that they want the best for me too. I don't think I could bear to be away from you. My days here are numbered anyway."

"But you may not even remember me once you go back," Rook suggested.

"Do you want me to go home? Am I burdening your life? You're tired of protecting me aren't you?" Her face heated up as if tears would come. They did not.

Rook wrapped his arms around her shoulders pressing the side of his cheek to hers. "That's not it—at all! I'm worried I may not be worth sacrificing your old life for." Rook continued to hold her close. Not because she needed it but because *he* did.

"I'm sure Alexa is probably getting frustrated with my world by now," Gwen agreed.

Rook's expression turned more hopeless—his arms felt heavier with sudden weakness. Gwen pushed him back from her to get a look at his face. "What aren't you telling me?" Gwen accused, "You know something."

Rook knew there was no denying it.

Gwen shook his shoulders and tried to get him to make eye contact with her. "Rook! Tell me. I deserve to know."

Rook began, "I have just come into some new facts about the hunter and the wardlow legend."

"Oh? And when did this happen?" Gwen asked suspiciously.

"I've been having visions of Raven at night. I have heard her in my head speaking to me."

"Rook. This doesn't sound good. Has she come to you before I came along?" Gwen asked.

"No. I found that suspicious too. She said she didn't have time to explain. She said that you were dangerous and that I need to turn you over to the hunters."

Gwen's eyes widened. "You weren't actually considering it were you."

"No! I told her I couldn't do it and I wouldn't. Then the hospital thing happened. She said that the unsigned document was a warning and that if I don't comply, they will follow through next time. That could be today. I don't even know." Rook looked worried.

"Unsigned document? What are you talking about?" Gwen felt the cold sensation swirling in her center.

"Yeah. I thought you knew that too." Rook guaged her reaction before continuing.

"Oh wow! You don't know." Rook sighed. "Someone signed my signature to a package of documents giving permission to discontinue Raven's life-support!"

Oh my gosh! I have to tell him.

Rook took Gwen's look of tortured concern for a reaction to this news, which made him feel better about arguing her innocence with Raven.

"I just want to lay down and wake up when everything is all over with," Gwen said frustrated.

"Don't give up. We'll get through this. Everything is going to be fine," Rook assured.

"How can you say that? I'm a wardlow. There are hunters coming for me! This thing that we are fighting, you can't even see. What if they kill Raven? Do you think I can live with that?"

"So what? Turn yourself in? Then what? Do you think whoever is holding Raven is just going to let her go? Why is she being held captive? How? By whom?" Rook sighed. "You aren't the only one fighting this battle."

Gwen paused and dazed for a moment before continuing, "I am in a lose/lose situation. I am finding it really hard to focus on the bright side of things. By the end of this I will have lost it all; one way or another. I may even get killed in the process. Right now, that seems like the best possible scenario."

Rook hugged her, "Don't think like that. You are going to have to toughen up for the fight ahead. You're too stubborn to lay down and die. I know you better than that," Rook reasoned, "If you know you are going to lose everything, then what are you afraid of? Don't fear the inevitable."

"If I turn myself in, it might save Raven, the hunters won't come for you, and I will either die or go home. I won't have to worry anymore. It will be over and we can move on. Why drag this out? We know this is going to end badly no matter what."

"You can't know that for sure. This switch is only temporary. You could wake in your bed tomorrow."

Gwen couldn't help but smile, "yeah and Alexa can wake up in your bed tomorrow."

Rook chuckled at the thought. "Serves her right for bringing you into this mess." He shook his head. "That's the

Gwen I like to see."

"Why would they do such a thing? What do they want with me so badly? I didn't ask for any of this! I just wanted to go home and be with my family. I didn't want to drag you into this mess. I am so sorry!"

"She said that they will send you back to your world, unharmed."

Why would they threaten Rook's sister in order to get to me? They must fear me. Why else manipulate those around me? Is the Raven Rook sees the same Raven I saw?

"Rook. This doesn't make any sense," Gwen said warily looking to the ground.

Rook gave her a confused glance and continued walking. He could see she had words on the tip of her tongue ready to spill over.

"That's—what I need to talk to you about," Gwen finally spit out. "I—uh..." Gwen swallowed hard. "I—uh—didn't tell you everything."

Rook's heart felt like a 20-pound bolder sinking in his chest. He wanted to cut her off and start lecturing her about how she promised not to keep any more secrets but decided against it. "It's almost two. How about you tell me after the meeting?"

Gwen sighed a breath of relief. She was in no hurry to break the news to him.

Chapter Sixteen

On their way to the secret meeting location, Gwen took time to reflect on what she saw while in the calm.

Invisible to the world she stood by Raven's bedside, adjacent from where Rook sat playing the guitar and singing his heart out.

A whirlwind of admiration swirled in her center. She felt a bond to the beautiful comatose young girl laying before her. Suddenly, she felt an internal spinning. Though the room stood still before her, she felt as if she was spinning inside of herself. Following the spinning sensation was a pressure on her semi-formless presence, the pressure pulled her forward. Feeling as if she would fall forward onto Raven's bed—as if gravity was shifting.

Falling onto the bed clumsily and confused she attempted to push herself back. The pull grew stronger and wind blew through her. Raven's body became a magnetic force which drew her inward. Gwen fought the pull as long as she could before surrendering to it.

Gwen felt as if she were falling out of an airplane. The wind blew past her, drag force collided against her semi-formless body. Though she was pulled forward, she was suddenly falling backward.

Her surroundings no longer consisted of the hospital setting. Now she saw the dark stormy sky rumbling in front of her, as she fell backward. The falling sensation slowed and it felt as if she were floating. Her vision went black for a moment before she saw the desolate sandy place.

Gwen spun around to see the emptiness. Within her center she felt hollow and cold. "Why am I here?" she yelled frustrated. "Can anyone hear me?" Gwen was surprised to hear herself aloud. *I think I'm getting the hang of this.*

A voice called from behind. She spun around to see who it was. In the distance, much further away than she expected was a small figure approaching. The figure was cloaked in bright white. Straight black hair spilled out in layers from the sides of the hood of her cloak.

"What do you want with me?" Gwen asked.

"It is you who came to me," the figure said.

"It was an accident."

"No such thing," the figure replied as it approached.

"Where did you come from? We are surrounded by nothing."

"Because you see nothing does not mean there is nothing to see," the figure responded. "No one sees everything and therefore, we are all blind."

The figure finally stood within ten feet of Gwen. She raised her hood to reveal herself.

"Raven?" Gwen asked stammering, "How?"

"I'm not really here. Just as you are not really here."

"You are in the hospital with Rook," Gwen explained.

"No. I am being held captive by the formless in the WOTU. They are trying to tap into my energy source to take form in our world. We cannot allow that to happen."

"How can we stop it?"

"You have to tell my brother to pull the plug."

"What? I can't do that!" Fire churned in Gwen's center now.

"Once they capture the spectrum wardlows, they will use my body as a portal the way you have used it to travel here. I am the prism cell. They will use me as a universal key to vacate souls from their bodies. Those souls will be held captive to provide the white light for future generations."

"So, let's stop it! Don't let them use your body."

"There is nothing we can do to stop it. They are too powerful. They have been planning this for centuries," Raven explained.

"Besides killing you, what needs to happen to prevent this?"

"You must keep them from collecting all ROYGBIV spectrum souls which are most easily taken from wardlows. This is easiest because of their arrangement with TAS. This will allow them to activate the prism cell and generate the white light needed to access *any* body."

"What spectra are left to collect?"

"BIV are the most complicated for them to collect. The higher the wave frequency, the more complex the abilities. You are a V-spectrum. My brother is an I-spectrum."

"But he isn't a wardlow."

"Wardlows are not what you think they are. Unfortunately, I don't have time to explain. You will likely figure it out someday," Raven said. "Your soul is of the V-spectrum, and you have a lot to learn."

"So, what spectrum are you?"

"As a prism cell, I am all and none."

"That makes no sense," Gwen argued.

"And it probably never will," Raven stated.

"I don't know what to do. I just want to go home."

"You are closer to home than you know."

Gwen's ears began to ring before her surroundings faded to black.

Gwen heard the gasps as she and Rook came down the stairs. No special ability needed, to read their anger, frustration and fear.

"Everybody stay calm!" Gwen demanded. "Rook is a part of our team now."

"You don't get to make those decisions on your own! Especially, something so reckless!" Hui-ming said—outraged.

"From now on, I make my own decisions! You may influence my decisions but I have the final say. I didn't ask to be a part of this. Now that I am, I will play my part to the best of my capabilities."

"How can we trust you to play your part? All you had to do was blend in and not expose your true nature! You can't even handle that!" Hui-ming exclaimed.

"Rook saved my life and this entire operation, so I suggest you show some respect for saving your lame bottoms too! A hunter came for me. Were any of you there?" Gwen wasn't really asking the question, "No. You weren't. Rook was. He brought me to safety—running from a force he couldn't see, no questions asked. I told him what I know about myself—which isn't much. I haven't told him about any of you. He has been contacted by a partially visible force claiming that if he turns me into the hunters, I can go home unharmed but Alexa's life would be forfeit."

"Out of the question!" Cat jumped out of her chair and pounded the table in front of her.

"I know that! But they are onto him, and so we must bring him into the mission."

Jazz eyed Rook approvingly, "You are alright with

what's going on?"

"I'm as alright as one can expect to be. I care about Gwen's safety."

"But what of Alexa's? Not to be crass but we would do anything to bring Alexa back safely."

"I care more about getting her back than any of you do —I can sense that. But I also care about saving my own behind—something you could care less about, which is why Rook and I will be involved in every little detail of the plan. He can show me how to blend."

"What is a V-spectrum Wardlow? Anyone?" Gwen's eyes shifted to Pico and Hui-ming. They exchanged glances. Gwen took that to mean they had no idea. "Rook's vision told him they can't find me the way they find other wardlows because I'm on the ultraviolet spectrum. What does that mean?"

Pico spoke up now, "Well, the ultraviolet spectrum is a wave frequency. We have never heard the classification before. Perhaps it has something to do with the serum?"

"They say I'm dangerous and that because I'm a V-spectrum wardlow, I can see the hunters coming. This weakens their defenses and they cannot catch me as easily. They wanted Rook to turn me in. They seem weak and blind to me," Gwen said with confidence.

"They are trying to get tricky now. It sounds like you are on the same frequency as they are, allowing you to see them. You can't be in a higher frequency or they wouldn't be able to see you. I'm just speculating," Pico said. "Hui-ming, what do you think?"

"For the hunters, it's automatic to locate and subdue wardlows."

"Raven said she could get in trouble for talking to me about any of this and that the formless would kill her to get to me. They already tried to pull the plug on her life-support the other day. She said it was a warning."

"The formless?" Pico asked.

"What do you know?" Gwen asked. She sensed that he knew something. She could feel the room stiffen.

"The hunters are elite soldiers for the formless in the WOTU. If they have ulterior motives, as you suspect, you are in more danger than we thought. All of us are in danger." Pico was deep in thought now—looking through them. "I don't know enough. They come from a desolate world of hopelessness and emptiness. I've seen pictures of paintings from artists who claim to have seen into their world," Pico explained.

"Maybe we should talk to one of them?" Gwen suggested. She thought about the sketch Alexa kept in her drawer. *Was she one of the artists? Did any of her group know?*

The group gasped. Cat was the one to say it aloud, "Are you out of your mind? We are in enough danger thanks to your *coming out* party."

"Oh yeah. It's really all my fault. If I'm not mistaken, someone was supposed to have been there to pick me up the day I made the big leap!" Gwen said harshly.

Rook spoke up now, "Everything happens for a reason. Nothing can be undone now, so there is no point in wasting time bickering over it."

"Rook is right," Jazz commented.

Gwen wanted to tell them about her meeting with Raven but decided against it. *This is not the way he should find out.*

"I will help her any way I can. We have gathered some of Alexa's items for research." Rook added with confidence. A part of him felt good about playing the protective role again—big brother and now husband, soon to be widow. He shook the thought from his mind. Some how, some way, this all had to work out. Even after all he has been through—losing his family—he refused to let go of the belief. His mother insisted on these values and he would not let them go. *Mom was always right in the end, no matter how long it took, she was always right.* Rook never suspected he would love for someone as much as he loved for his own family.

"We will meet again tomorrow. You two go now, see what you can find. We will work out a schedule for tomorrow and reconvene after we have thought about what you told us. Keep your phone close."

The car ride was silent. Both of them contemplated the overwhelming state of things. The rest of the day was spent digging through more files and objects of interest. After a long dreamless sleep Gwen decided to tell Rook the truth before she had time to chicken out. *He trusts me. I don't want to lose that. Besides, we are part of a team with a purpose beyond protecting ourselves.* She didn't waste another second. Before saying so much as good morning she began, "Raven and I met in the desolate dark place. The one from my nightmare."

Rook's eyes widened. "What did she say?"

"She was... uh... explaining how we have to prevent the formless from using her body as a portal to our world."

"What?" Rook spit out.

"She told me to tell you to pull the plug," Gwen said just above a whisper.

Rook backed away from Gwen as if she were contagious. "This can't be! She was right. You *are* the enemy."

"No. I'm just telling you what I saw. I tried to reason

179

with her. I told her there has to be another way to prevent it from happening," Gwen defended.

"So what if the formless come here? The hunters are already here. What difference does it make?" Rook yelled.

"They are going to take form here. They plan to use our bodies as vehicles. They are going to corrupt this world!"

"No. That is the wardlows purpose—*your* purpose," Rook accused.

"That isn't true and you know it!" Gwen defended angrily.

"You need to go home. Stay away from me and my family!" Rook yelled.

Gwen's expression melted with her heart and suddenly she felt sick. She closed the gap between them to touch him. "After all of the time we spent together! I can't believe you would throw it all away," Gwen argued. "This is why I should have kept my mouth shut. I told you the truth against my better judgment and look what has happened. The forces have turned you against me. I am the last piece of the puzzle, the most difficult spectrum to retrieve. And we are going to hand it over without a fight. This is exactly what they want."

"You aren't going to fool me again so you can forget it." Rook glared.

"Whatever. You will have to live with the consequences, not me. I won't be around to see how things play out!"

"I can't take anymore from you," Rook said bitterly. Pointing to the door, "Go now!" He swallowed hard, "Go now before I change my mind about turning you in."

Gwen turned around with her shoulders hunched. She felt as if she could curl up on the floor and die. She put her hand on the door to open it, "I can't do this alone." The words barely crept out, tears filled her eyes clouding her vision. "You don't have to turn me in. I will turn myself in,"

Gwen said sounding defeated.

Gwen's body went numb. "You know what? I don't care what you like anymore. It doesn't matter because I will be executed soon. Death will be a sweet release from the hurt your dishing me."

Rook rolled his eyes. His cheeks became a raging shade of red. "Oh stop. You don't love me. You are trying to kill what's left of my family."

"Why? What do I have to gain by killing her? Why would I do it? Did you ever stop to think that it makes no sense?"

"You feed off of my pain and are fueled by deceit. I'd drive you there myself but I'm afraid I might feel compelled to deliver justice myself." Rook yelled bitterly.

Chapter Seventeen

Gwen woke up cold and uncomfortable—her neck felt cramped. She had no recollection of falling asleep nor dreaming. Her body ached all over, as if covered in bruises. She opened her eyes and saw a few others confined with her. "Where am I? What's going on?"

One of the women spoke quietly, "We're awaiting trial."

"What? Trial? Oh no!"

"We are all in here for the same reason."

"What happens next?" Gwen asked.

"Trial, followed by execution. What else are they going to do with us? They aren't going to let us populate the planet. We are sadistic, barbaric people," the woman said rolling her eyes sarcastically.

Gwen looked at the woman with shock. "I don't remember how I got here."

"You were probably turned over by one of your friends or a family member."

"He wouldn't do that." Gwen said defensively but her center twisted with despair at the memory of his words—his threat to turn her in. The hate in his eyes when he said it.

"Well you would have remembered encountering a hunter. I know I gave him a good fight. Not bad for a blind fight." She smirked in admiration at the memory. "Oh, don't worry, whomever outed you will more than likely be sitting out front at trial. At least you won't die not knowing who betrayed you."

The words began to sink in. *I'm going to die soon. No more Rook, no more grandparents, no more Alexa.* "Wait a minute! I heard that once a wardlow is executed, their soul returns to the world from which it came."

The girl gave her a suspicious look up and down, "Where did you get that load of garbage from—*pro-wardlow.org?* They don't care what happens to our soul. As far as they are concerned, we have no soul. And once they show the jury what they have seen with their own eyes, they won't be sympathetic either!" The woman looked disgusted by Gwen's optimism. "We are caught, it's over. You might want to use the last moments of your life to say your prayers."

The other alleged wardlows stood silent and dazed—lifeless behind their eyes. Gwen wondered if there was a difference between them and herself.

"There has to be something we can do! Don't any of you have any special abilities of good use?" Gwen pleaded in a panic.

"What do you think these neck braces are for?" The woman's eyes widened with aggravation.

"The neck braces began to hum with electricity." A guard walked past the cell of wardlows and zipped his lips at them. "The trial begins now. If you speak or so much as whisper, you will regret it."

These braces aren't to prevent abilities! They are to prevent us from communicating or starting a riot!

"Before a jury of our peers we will witness proof that the folks we have gathered before you are no longer within their natural form. Their bodies used as a host for the wardlow to unleash its corruption onto our pure lands."

Gwen wondered how they would prove such a thing. *This definitely sounds like an execution hearing, rather than a simple evacuation process. Why would Raven lie to Rook about such a thing? It has to be a trick.* Gwen wanted to protest but couldn't. The collar around her neck pulsed with a charge. She could hear it in her ears. *If I so much as clear my throat the collar will shock me senseless. Oh they would like that. The only thing the witnesses would see is me shaking in panic and they would automatically consider me guilty. The guards would say I was resisting arrest and take me down on the spot—problem solved.* This is not something she would expect from Rook's people but she couldn't help but suspect it now. *Fear does things to people. It brings out the animal instinct in us all.*

Gwen had no idea how she was going to get out of this mess. It wasn't just herself she worried about. *What about the other innocent people beside me? Are they just like me? Did they too travel from another world to this place? Maybe they came from somewhere else altogether. Maybe they are dangerous.* Some wore expressions of disgust, while others looked hopeless and unwilling to fight for justice.

"Once our findings have been confirmed by these witnesses, they will be removed from our world forever and their friends and family may begin the traditional mourning process. May the creator bless them during this time of great loss."

Gwen's eyes widened, her mind raced as the ice cold sensation spread from her shoulders down to the tips of her fingers. *They will kill her! Alexa will not be able to return to her body if they destroy it! This will trap her in my world forever! They don't care what happens to either of us! Why would they? Oh my gosh! This is how they intend to collect the V-spectrum! They plan to capture Alexa once they execute her body. The other Raven is a fake! She may try to collect Rook's soul next. But how? It doesn't matter now—there is nothing I can do. Check-mate. I'm totally screwed!*

"Bring the first wardlow forth unto the chamber."

Two guards walked one of the women to a large clear crystal pillar-shaped chamber, just big enough for one person. One guard opened the crystal sidewall where shackle hooks hung. The guards clicked and snapped the shackle contraption allowing the chains between her wrists to be displaced further apart.

"Step onto the platform miss," a guard requested. The other guard gave him a disgusted look.

"Do not speak kindly to this abomination! It is a filthy parasite who came here to enslave us all!" The guard rolled his eyes. Gwen thought he must rank higher than the other guard.

The sound of thick chains trudging down the hallway echoed loudly. Gwen's eyes widened with a few exaggerated blinks. *Baylee? It can't be!* Gwen panicked.

"This one almost escaped," The guard said with fury in his eyes.

"She should go next then!" another guard responded.

Baylee had given both guards looks of utter disgust. Baylee looked like a fighter—something Gwen had never known her to be. She looked as though she had a score to settle. If not for the shock band around her neck, Gwen was willing to bet her life that Baylee would have spat in one of their faces. Most likely the guard who suggested she be the next in line.

Baylee stepped onto the clear crystal platform on the concave side of the door. The guards pulled the right hand to the right shackle hook and the left hand to the left shackle hook. Gwen heard another metal latch behind the door as the chain tightened around her waist. *Wow! We must be really dangerous! Precisely what they want the witnesses to think,* Gwen thought and then wondered if this chamber was a torture device.

Is this the last footstep I'll ever take in this perfect world? The last mile of all roads ahead? She was curious about what proof they had against them all. *I am no danger to this world. I didn't choose to come here. I did nothing wrong! I can't die now. I have too many unanswered questions.*

The guards covered her eyes with what looked like a thick pair of glasses. Baylee squirmed as they were set in place. Gwen listened closely as the guard explained to her, "You will be unable to blink once the chamber is activated. You will experience a little discomfort but no pain. Your eyes will feel dry afterward. Eye drops will be administered to dilate your eyes. The lubrication drops, which are thick but soothing, will be administered before and after the process." This was the nicer of the two guards —Gwen sensed his compassion.

Gwen's curiosity peaked as she wondered what memories would be revealed. *Could it really be her?* The chamber started humming a low, almost, inaudible tone. Baylee's skin began to glow a beautiful blue tint and then her back jolted into an arch. Gwen saw the lenses in front of her eyes filled with the blue tint; they were like projectors. The projection from the small lenses enlarged exponentially after refracting through the crystal chamber and onto the wall for the witnesses to see.

Random images flashed onto the projection screen. A minute passed and the images slowed. A short segment of a video from Baylee's memories looped—repeated as the man spoke. "As you can see here, this memory is of people being shot to death in mass quantities. This memory is animals killing each other, witnessed by the wardlow. Hundreds of thousands of footage of her consuming various items: plants, butchered animals, water, fruit from trees. Our claims are proven clearly and we ask that you agree to execution.

Gwen was astounded by the proof. *Is that all they need to prove guilt?* Baylee's memories were from television shows she watched. *She didn't witness any of those things.* Gwen was thankful to have not been a fan of television. *Not that it matters, I can't deny eating and drinking. She doesn't even get to tell her side of the story?* Gwen could not stand the thought of watching Baylee's execution. *I don't understand how she physically manifested in this world, but it is her. Her eyes are different and her physical appearance shows no flaws but otherwise she is the spitting image of her former self.* Gwen caught a glimpse of familiar images during Baylee's trial.

"Move her to the holding area. Quickly please, we have got at least eight of these worthless pieces of meat to go through."

"Meat sir?" the other guard asked curiously.

"It's a word these savages use to refer to the animals they kill, mutilate and consume!"

Gwen knew her number was almost up. She thought about all of the things the machine would reveal about her. She dreaded that Rook might see her do the things this world considered despicable, disgusting, and unforgivable. She was more anxious about this than the execution.

A breeze blew across her face as the door swung open—she felt more claustrophobic than ever. Sounds outside of the chamber were muffled. Her breath did not fog the glass. The inside of the chamber was cool and refreshing. Despite the shackles she was comfortable.

Gwen shifted her eyes to the audience—the witnesses—the jury she guessed. *Oh man! He's here. If he thought he hated me before, he will really hate me after he sees how barbaric my memories are. I'm sorry for failing you Alexa. I see now why this is so important to you.* Gwen thought time had slowed down upon entering the chamber. *I just want to get this over with.*

The drops were administered, goggles put into place. Though her vision was blurry, the images projected onto the screen were visible. She cringed but only for a brief moment. *I don't recognize any of these memories! These have to be Alexa's memories! How?*

Gwen watched memories of Alexa as a child, as a teen, as a student. No memories of consumption nor violence. The man grumbled as he stumbled through Alexa's memory-banks as if he had inserted an incorrect DVD. "This has to be a mistake," he said quietly. "Pardon me folks, we appear to be experiencing technical difficulties." The man turned the machine off and called his technicians to look at the pillar. Gwen heard the man ask someone what was going on, "Are you sure she is one of them?"

"I am sure. I am viewing her memories now. She is a wardlow. There must be something wrong with the machine!"

The technicians found no problems with the machine.

"Put her back among the pack. Let's proceed to the next trial and see if we get the same result."

Too early to get excited, she thought. *I don't know what's happening but I'm thankful for the delay. The man can see my memories but the machine cannot. Interesting.* Gwen hoped the technicians were done looking for the problem. *Maybe it's the V-spectrum thing.*

The next five trials were successful in proving the wardlow's guilt.

"Bring the redhead again," the man demanded.

They went through the trouble of strapping her into the machine and found the same result. "Because this case cannot be proven, we have no choice but to release this woman. Does the jury agree?" Jury gave the thumbs up. Rook was among them but Gwen could not see his face. Gwen wondered what expression he wore at this moment.

The guards apologized as they removed the shackles and band from her neck. "This has never happened before. TAS are flawless in their findings."

"What if they haven't been? What if they have their own ulterior motives for executing our people?" Gwen asked.

"It's no wonder they picked you up. You can't go around saying stuff like that, it sounds nuts."

Gwen agreed with him for the sake of getting out of there. "What's going to happen to the others? I know they are being executed, but when?"

"They are held for three days in case there is a last minute appeal."

Gwen mentally rolled her eyes at the man, "How many of those are actual successes?"

"I know. But they still have rights as our people. They get that final chance to fight."

Gwen wondered if this world have ever heard of double-jeopardy.

"You will have to find a ride home quickly or stay here. It's going to be dark soon."

"I'm not sure where home is right now. Somebody wrongly accused me and that is how I ended up here. I don't know who it was."

"That was an awful thing to do. It seems like if they cared for you at all they would make pretty darn sure you were guilty," the guard said appalled. "I'm sorry you had to go through that tonight. It must have been terrifying."

"Did I have a mobile phone when I was brought in?

Can you tell me anything about what happened? I sure would appreciate it," Gwen asked hopeful.

"I will see what I can find out."

"You know what? I think I will just stay here tonight. Where will I stay?"

"We don't want you sleeping with the wardlows. We have never had a case of innocence but we do have a nice room to accommodate workers. Some like to take a nap between shifts."

"They won't mind?"

"After what you've been through, who cares?"

Rook pulled Gwen aside in the hallway away from the passing guards. "What just happened?"

"Rook! Oh my gosh! What are you doing here?" Gwen asked happy to see him and then her tone changed. "Did you come to see me executed—make sure I got what I deserved?"

Rook's smile flipped reflexively in defense. "No. Of course not!"

"Then why did you turn me over to them? Why are you here?" Gwen was fuming.

"What? I didn't turn you in." Rook said offended. "How could you even think that?"

"You told me you wanted nothing to do with me. You even offered to drive me when I told you I was going to turn myself in! I won't even repeat what you said after that!"

"I was mad. It was a protective reflex. I didn't mean any of it." Then something clicked into place. "So, wait—you didn't turn yourself in?"

"I don't remember anything. The last thing I remember is our argument. I didn't know where to go so I headed for the secret meet location. If nobody was there I was just going to sit & sulk for a bit until I figured out what to do next. I wanted to die Rook. Do you understand how bad you hurt me?"

Rook cringed at the memory. "Let's get out of here before someone overhears us or changes there minds about letting you go." Then he thought to ask, "What happened anyway?"

"I'm innocent," Gwen said astounded. All anger dissipated.

"That's what they said but how?"

"I don't know. Those memories weren't mine."

"So, you aren't a wardlow?"

"TAS says that I *am*. He thinks the machine is faulty. It's probably because I am only synthetic. Who the heck knows?"

"So, are you ready to get out of here before they change their mind?" Rook asked upbeat and glad the chase was over.

"No. Actually, I told the guard I had nowhere to go tonight and they agreed to let me stay here."

"What? Are you insane?" Rook yelled at a whisper.

"I can't leave them here," she whispered. "I can't leave *her* here," Gwen added.

"Who?"

"Baylee."

"Baylee? Are you delusional?"

"I thought so at first but no. She is a wardlow."

"That's impossible."

"I told you *impossible* would become part of your vocabulary." Gwen shook her head. "I won't lose her again."

"So, what's your plan?"

"I think you know."

"Haven't you had enough excitement for one month?"

"If I can get them out of here in time I'm going to bring them home."

"I have a better idea," Rook said knowing better than to argue.

Gwen looked at Rook warily expecting him to say something against her grain.

"Bring them to the sanctuary. Do you remember the way?"

"I do. It is one of my favorite memories," Gwen smiled.

Rook eyes became more sincere. "Well if you plan to make it before sunrise you had better get going."

"I need something from you before you go."

"Anything."

"You see the braces on the wardlow's necks?"

"Of course."

"I need a key. Can you manifest one?"

Rook gazed ahead in contemplation. "I'm sorry. I am unfamiliar with the device. I can't help you there."

Gwen sighed.

"Gwen. Are you sure about this? The odds of getting them out safely..." He shook his head.

"I have to try."

Rook put his hands on Gwen's waist and kissed her forehead. "Do what you feel you have to. Please be careful."

"Of course." Gwen smiled.

They turned from one another and began to part ways when Rook called to her. "Oh I forgot to tell you..."

Gwen turned around.

"I found this in Alexa's stuff. I forgot about it during our argument."

Rook held a palm-sized black reflective disc flat in his palm. Gwen picked up the disc and held it up at eye level.

"What is it?" Gwen asked amazed by the reflective

surface of the object. It felt cool to the touch like stone.

"I don't know. It looks like some kind of black mirror." Rook shrugged. "Hang onto it for good luck and think of me."

"If I think about you while I do this I'm going to get distracted and get us all caught," Gwen joked.

"I will wait for you at the sanctuary. If you're not there by sunrise, I will rest there until you do arrive."

Gwen shook her head and smiled at him. "I'd say, don't wait up but I don't want to jinx myself."

"See you soon then," Rook said before giving her that last look—reminding her of Mimic before he met with his counselor.

"Soon. Yes," Gwen agreed.

Chapter Eighteen

Gwen was impressed with her accommodations for the evening. The bed was nice, the overhead dome large with some sort of shade covering the hole. The wall colors a dark bold red with subtle golden vertical patterns. The large bedspread a matching warm earth-tone golden embroidered diamond patterns. *This reminds me of a high class suite for royalty.* Paintings hung on the walls, statues sat in the corners. The shades were partially drawn to keep the room lit. A cozy looking desk stood against the wall across from the bed.

"The shades are all remote control. When you are ready to turn in for the evening simply press this button and the shades will open supplying you with an abundant source of sunshade for the evening. I do hope you will enjoy your stay. Again, we sincerely apologize for the misunderstanding. I can't imagine what it must have felt like having your life on display for all to see."

"It's quite alright. You are just doing what you have to do to protect the people. And a mighty thorough job I might add. Thank you for accommodating me so kindly. This room is beautiful."

Shortly after the guard left Gwen peaked out of the room to see if any guards were watching. *No one is keeping an eye on me because I'm no longer a suspect. I'm sure the holding area is well patrolled.* Her instincts guided her through the long hallways.

Gwen cracked the door open and saw the holding area

was not patrolled. Not even so much as a surveillance camera on the premise. *For such an advanced civilization, these guys sure are behind in technology.* The prisoners neckbands were not lit up but they were still intact. *That could get uncomfortable after a few days. Sleeping in them was certainly no treat.*

"What are you doing here?" a prisoner asked.

"I'm going to get you out of here. All of you," Gwen explained.

"Why would you do that? We're wardlows."

"So am I," Gwen admitted.

"No you aren't. I saw what happened. Your memories are clean."

"How did you fool the machine?" another prisoner asked.

"I don't know how it happened but I'm not going to leave you guys here because I was able to beat it, we are a team, we have to stick together. I am part of something—a small underground group fighting for people like us. Alexa is fighting against the system, trying to find a way to fix us."

"Fix us? What exactly do they think is wrong with us?"

"Alexa and her group is trying to find a way to put us back in our world which would bring back their people. She doesn't believe our souls corrupt or consume the souls of the initial inhabitants. She believes it's more like a swap; a trading places sort of thing."

"How the heck do you intend to prove such a thing?"

"I'm not sure what her plan is. I am an innocent bi-stander. I am what they call an induced v-spectrum wardlow. Alexa injected herself with a chemical, which brought about the swap and here I am." The wardlow prisoners listened in awe.

"So this chemical? Can it send us back home?"

"I don't know much about it yet. As far as I know, the

change is temporary, it was designed as a means of research, to relate and create a sort of antidote or immunization for it—one that will not harm either soul."

"Well that's great news! We might survive after all."

"The only problem is, the inventor of the formula is no longer with us. He was killed by a panicked wardlow. The secret died with him. His daughter, Alexa, is desperate to connect the dots and finish what he started. She will need your help once we switch back, which could be any minute, day, week or month. I don't know what we will remember so it is important that I have a group of people that I can trust to help her when she returns. I will do whatever I can to help while I am here," Gwen explained.

"How do you plan to get us out of here?"

"I haven't worked out the details yet. I know where we're going but I'm not sure how we're going to get there. I will get you out of here. I promise! I will return once I think this through. Hang in there, get to know each other and think about what I have told you."

Gwen closed the door and began her journey back to her luxurious suite. Halfway down the hallway she heard a loud knocking sound along the walls followed by a grinding, mechanical sound. The blinds along the walls were shut to keep the hallway lit. Darkness crept up from the floor as the blinds began to rise. Gwen's veins felt icy as she began to run. *Keep your cool Gwen. Remember where your room is.* She attempted to calm herself so she wouldn't lose her way. Her legs disappeared in the darkness which crawled up her waistline. Running as fast as Alexa's body would allow, Gwen knew she wouldn't make it back to her room in time. Picking up the pace she ran at full capacity. As the darkness spread to her cheekbones, her eyes glanced down at the visually impenetrable black void beneath her. The blackness made her feel paralyzed. Unable to see her legs in motion below was disorienting.

The door handles on the adjacent wall were now engulfed in darkness. Getting back to the room was only the half the battle. She wondered how she could save the prisoners now. *I made a promise and I don't intend to break it.* Deep in thought, she tripped over something solid on the floor stubbing her toe. She fell to the ground in the black hole, which engulfed the room. *No sense in running anymore.* She sat against a wall as the stun from her toe faded.

Sitting in complete darkness Gwen considered her options. Her head felt heavy on top of her neck. Her temples began to ache. She reached for her face to feel if her eyes were open or closed. Pulling her fingers down her face she pushed her eyelids in the down position and then pinched the corners of her eyes together to alleviate some pressure. Suddenly, visions flooded her mind in rapid successions. The darkness in front of her gone; replaced by memories, which were not her own. They weren't Alexa's either. The thoughts flooded her mind painfully as if some kind of mind levy broke wide open.

As the hallucinations slowed it felt more like a slide-show of still frames mixed with short segments of motion picture. With plenty of time on her hands she calmed herself and patiently watched the mental slide-show. Then she saw the same memory from various points of perspective. An image of herself in the crystal chamber and the inability to prove her guilt. The memories were from the jury, which surrounded the crystal chamber. *This memory must have made an impression on all of them. How am I seeing these? Why?*

Suddenly, a memory she could use—one of the guards patrolling the hallway. *Could it really be that simple?* She stood up in the pitch black hallway. In touch with the memory Gwen somehow managed to willingly hold in her mind as she took steps in sync with her mental vision. Instinctively, she held her hand out to the wall of doors for guidance. As she stepped forward in her mind, she stepped forward in the darkness. As she saw the doors in her mind, she reached for the door handles in the darkness—calibrating her sensory perception with that of reality. As she passed each door, she felt more confident. She held her excitement at bay to prevent the gift from fleeing. The headache was no longer a nuisance—it had been a life-saver.

Gwen made it back to her suite safely. She closed the door, closed her eyes, and let out a deep sigh. When she opened her eyes again, everything looked the way it had before leaving. She tapped out of the guard's memories effortlessly. She sat at the desk, rested her forehead in her hand; fingers laced in her thick hair. *How am I going to do this? I can't be sure this memory ability will work. Will they trust me to get them out? What choice would they have? They will be executed anyway. They will execute me for attempting to rescue them.* Gwen took another 20 minutes to calm her nerves.

Gwen's head filled with ideas. The speed and capacity of such ideas seemed impossible. *Did I get this ability from the crystal chamber? I can read the memories of everyone within the machines proximity. The machine read Alexa's memories. Does that mean I can tap into them too? I wonder...*

Gwen opened the desk drawer to see what was in it, "A stapler, that will work." She set the stapler on the desktop and closed the drawer. "What to try, oh what to try?" She thought for a moment, "What do I need to pull this off?" It was so obvious that she wanted to smack herself. *A key to open the wardlow holding area would be nice.* Then she reconsidered, *Oh I know. I need to deactivate and release the neck braces. Those things have got to be rigged so magic, or whatever they call it, doesn't work on them. I will need the real deal.*

Gwen put her hand on the stapler, closed her eyes, and reached through the memories until she found the one she was looking for—a means to unlocking the neck devices. *I'm not sure how to do this,* she followed her instincts and hoped for the best. She focused on the device; its weight, its shape, and the knowledge the guard had stored in his memory. Gwen was so in tune with the vision that she could feel the device in her hand. The memory was so clear that she was sure she knew how to use the device. Her center filled with confidence, so she let the memory slip into a dark point, far in the distance of her mind.

"It worked!" Gwen's eyes widened to the fullest of their capacity. She had to keep from jumping out of her chair and screaming with excitement. Rook's abilities were now Gwen's and she was able to combine abilities. She thought about the day Rook explained it to her. Similar size, similar elemental properties. *I'd better not get too excited yet. I can't say for sure this thing works. If not for the memory ability I would have encountered the same problems Rook had earlier.*

Gwen peaked out to see the dark hallways were just as dark as before. *The darkness could be my best ally.* She wanted to believe the wardlows were desperate enough to follow her blindly in the dark, but a part of her warned that this plan might not go so smoothly. Time was ticking, anxiety resonated in her center. *Now is the time, you can't afford to stall any longer.* Without delay, she ran silently down the halls confident, even in darkness. She knew her steps well enough.

Gwen paused at the door where the wardlows were

held captive. She didn't want to panic them by opening the door in complete darkness. *What if they start screaming or something?* Gwen pushed her last-minute worries aside. *This is it! Don't chicken out now!* she argued with herself. *Once you open this door, there is no turning back,* her mind warned.

Gwen heard a voice in her mind, which was not her own, *"We are waiting for you. Don't just stand there."*

What? Gwen thought.

"It's Teka, I can communicate telepathically. Come on, we are waiting for you."

I wish I would have known that earlier. She cracked the door open hoping the room would be lit. To Gwen's surprise, the room was lit. I guess they wouldn't care about wardlow nourishment. A thought hit Gwen like a ton of bricks, *This is how they execute them! They let their bodies starve!*

One of the wardlow men spoke up, "Have you found a way to get us out of here?"

Gwen sighed, "I can get you out of here but you will have to trust me. The hallways are completely filled with sunshade. I can navigate them but you will all be blind."

"Not all of us," a young boy said. Gwen's heart broke at the sight of his beautiful little face. He continued, "I can see day or night. Not the same way, but I get by."

The wardlows gasped. "That's amazing!" one of the woman said quietly.

"What about these?" the woman pointed to her neck-brace.

"I think I can take care of those," Gwen said pulling the make-shift device out of her pocket, giving the prisoners a glimpse before quickly stuffing it back down into her pocket.

A man's eyes widened at the sight of the device, "How did you get your hands on that!"

"Shh..." Gwen exclaimed. "It doesn't matter. I just hope it works." Gwen took a deep breath reluctant to open the holding cell. "I'm going to open this door but you all have to promise me you aren't going to flee or do anything stupid. If one of us gets caught, we all get caught. We have to work together. We have to trust each other. Understood?"

The wardlows nodded.

"Have you worked out a plan? We won't be safe anywhere we go. They can see our minds. They know where we have been," a woman warned.

"You are right," Gwen answered. "The sunshade will work to our advantage." Gwen put her hand on the opening of the door. "You can't see where you are going, so there is no memory trail for them to follow. They can tap my memory but it will mislead them. I don't know how long this will stall them, but it's worth the risk. They will know I'm involved. Next time, I won't have this advantage, so I suggest you all do the best you can to stay out of sight. If you stay together," Gwen pointed to the young boy, "he should be able to guide you through the darkness, to a new location."

"Marr," the boy said. "My name is Marr."

Baylee argued, "But they will just read his memories won't they?"

"That is why you must keep moving."

Gwen put her hand on the lock and turned it to dust. She pulled the device back out of her pocket and used it on the first neck brace. It opened with a clanking sound. Each prisoner had the same reflex upon removal of their braces—rubbing and rotation of the neck.

"Marr, can you drive in the sunshade? I mean, can you fully navigate with your unique sight?"

Marr shook his head. "I can. But where will we get a car? We are going to need a few cars or a van we can all cram into."

"We'll cross that bridge when we come to it," Gwen said.

Some of the wardlows looked worried and hopeless; looking at the ground and shaking their heads.

"Trust guys. I told you; you have to trust. This is our only chance. If anyone argues, it will slow us down and we cannot afford delay. Once we are on the move that's it. The minute someone notices you are gone, panic will emerge, and they will have all of their forces on the lookout. Do not make me have to leave you behind. I will if I must.

Chapter Nineteen

The wardlows put all of their faith in the strange wardlow girl leading them down the dark hallway. Gwen requested Marr close his eyes before leaving the room while she led them down the hallway via borrowed memories. She alternated between the guards' memories to deflect their trail. She wasn't sure how well it would work, but her instincts told her it would.

Though the hallways were dark with several turns the wardlows moved at a slow and steady pace, silently holding hands. The further they journey through the dark halls the more confident they became about their escape.

The line halted. Gwen used Teka's ability to communicate. *"We have to wait here a moment, there is no sunshade to hide behind ahead."* The wardlow's minds were as silent as the halls were dark.

Gwen looked around the room and saw a guard walk past. *I wonder...* Gwen thought. *Well, I sure hope this works because there is no room for error here.* Gwen focused on the guard walking past and tried to conjure Rook's ability, paired with TAS ability.

When the calm finally came, she triggered the gift of telepathy from Teka. *"I will go check things out. You must stay here, remain silent, and stay together."* Gwen walked out into the large lit room hoping to have taken on the form of the guard.

Upon entering the light she looked down at a sleeve and noticed it was, indeed, covered by uniform. "Excuse me sir, I am new here do you think you could show me around the main quadrant."

"Not a problem. It's great to see a woman join the force. We don't see many of them," the man said admirably. "You seem comfortable in your own skin if you don't mind me saying so." Gwen did her best to hold back a laugh at the irony.

"Thank you sir. That means a lot. I feel like a fish out of water right now," Gwen said.

"Takes some getting used to. You never know what you are going to get with these wardlows. They can be very unpredictable. Thank goodness for the neck braces," he said.

"The wardlows make you nervous eh? Have you ever witnessed an incident? Are they really that dangerous?"

"I haven't witnessed anything myself but a good friend of mine had the pleasure of encountering a very feisty one. He was executed on the spot." The man said tapping his left hand on his hip; a holster. *Could it be a gun?* "Not our proudest moment. We try to give everyone a fair shake at the system. But this particular wardlow was out of control and wouldn't listen to reason. The collar was ineffective and we were worried for our safety. We did what we felt we had to."

"Do the braces prevent them from using special abilities too?" Gwen asked.

"For the most part, they do. It depends on the ability. The braces cannot be manifested into something else. The key is required. The primary purpose for the neck brace is to keep them from speaking to one another and causing a scene at trial. Desperate wardlows will do whatever it takes to get free."

"Have any ever escaped the facility?" Gwen asked in a worried tone.

"Two or three have successfully gotten away from us.

Nobody knows how. Even TAS claims to have no insight to their escape. They are referred to as The All Seeing but I'll tell you, they don't see all things. They have blind-spots."

"How did we begin working with TAS? I'm not questioning authority here, but has anyone ever wondered if TAS and the WOTU people might have ulterior motives for the wardlow execution?"

"TAS are our protectors. They have only our best interest in mind. We don't question their motives. It's obvious to them, as it is obvious to us—we can't have those barbarians procreating on our lands and tainting the balance of perfection we have set. Our culture is abundant and without chaos. The wardlow mind is rotted by obsessions of material possession, aggressive behavior, selfishness, bitterness, and greed. They are parasitic in nature—they obsess over what they can get their hands on next."

"Wow! You know a lot about wardlows. I have to admit, my knowledge is limited to that of legends and bedtime stories. You must really despise them." Gwen milked for information.

"Actually, I don't. I think they are just unfortunate, terminally ill individuals."

"So, you probably aren't fond of the execution process then?" Gwen asked.

"None of us are. Well, one of us is."

"Yeah. I'm pretty sure I know who you are referring to," Gwen said thinking of the rude guard.

"He has a personal grudge against them. He lost his sister."

Gwen was sympathetic for the guard, how would he feel once he realized she could have been saved?

"Looking at her and then seeing the foreign memories in her head was so hard for him to witness. He had to see for himself to believe. He was in denial—like most family members are."

"Is anyone working on a possible cure for them?" Gwen asked hesitantly, hoping not to raise suspicion. I apologize for taking so much of your time with my questions."

"Ah. It's no problem. You have the same questions all new arrivals have. We don't perform tests on wardlows, it's immoral. I know that sounds crazy considering they are going to be executed. The friends and families of those afflicted would rather mourn their losses than take chances of wardlows mass-producing. Almost as if they are afraid of catching something from them."

"How much does society know about what goes on?"

"We try to keep things to a minimum and involve only the family and friends of the victims. They usually keep the affliction a secret, from shame I guess. We don't want to panic society. We are trying to prevent them from breeding and spreading. It isn't working though. Every year we find more and more of them. This is not the way evolution is supposed to work," he said frustrated.

"Aside from their dangerous memories, have they tried anything dangerous?" Gwen asked.

"It's not just their memories that are dangerous. Their ideas and insensitive nature could inspire and change the world as we know it. They are so very parasitic in the way they think—consume and abandon, consume and abandon, until nothing remains. I don't know what I'd do if my daughter were ever afflicted." The guard's eyes stared through Gwen rather than at her. She knew he was thinking of his daughter. She sensed the warmth of his adoration beaming from his skin. Gwen detected the faint aroma of roses.

Gwen returned to her new friends—the escapees. In the dark, with her telepathy she explained the plan. Adjusting the ability in her mind, like tuning in an old-fashioned radio. Finally, she heard their voices cutting in and out of her mind. *I don't think I can do this for very long. Too much going on,* she worried.

Gwen transformed the wardlow's clothing into that of in-house uniforms from different divisions. When the coast was clear, she pushed each wardlow from the dark hallway into the lit corridor. Each randomly walked around and then migrated inconspicuously to a dark area near the entrance of the building. Each hid in the shadows waiting for Gwen to lead them out of the building. She was the last one out into the open. Mentally navigating the escapee's fresh memories, she knew exactly where each of them hid. A few of them shared the same hiding spot.

Gwen used the memories from a guard to locate the entrance and learn of its security measures. Everything looked simple enough. Simple, until her built-in sensory perception warned that hunters were near. *More than one khaki man! Oh that's just great! There have to be at least three or four of them.* She panicked for a moment as she wondered how difficult it would be to use all of these abilities simultaneously. *Something has got to give right? Which ability will give first? I have to get them to safety before the hunters come! They aren't far.* The hunters' memories were off limits.

Gwen unlocked the front doors. She put the fear of the hunters in the back of her mind—just for now while she focused on her main objective.

Outside, she borrowed the boy's gift of sight. *What a messed up way of looking at things.* Sight didn't seem like the right word to describe the ability. Gwen managed to locate the vehicles. *A bus! Perfect!*

Carefully, she kept an eye on the corridor. She couldn't have anyone see her pulling people from the shadows. *The traffic in the corridor is minimal; not well patrolled. Why would it be?* She tapped her senses for the hunters periodically to gauge their proximity. They are much closer now. She tried not to show panic on her face, as she collected the wardlows from their hiding places.

She led the first three wardlows to Marr, from there he guided them onto the bus. *My plan is moving much smoother than anticipated; suspiciously smooth.*

Gwen waited alongside Teka in her dark hiding spot as guards walked past. One of the guards stopped and halted the other. Their words were too quiet to detect, and they were facing the opposite direction so lip reading was out of the question. Gwen's instincts twisted in her gut. *"This isn't good,"* she told Teka mentally.

"I sense it too. The atmosphere is thick."

"There are at least four more of us in hiding. This thing is about to spiral out of control. Keep the others calm. I will handle this. You have to get them to Marr before they lock the place down. You will all have to make a run for it. Make sure that Marr is ready to lead you to the van. Leave without me if you must. I will catch up. You know the location, relay it to Marr. Get there ASAP. Hunters are nearby, I can sense them. Move fast!"

"We can't do this without you."

"You can do it. Keep moving, don't get caught. I will do what I can to bury your tracks."

The guards showed signs of alert. Gwen wondered what set them off. She scanned all guard proximity and made rough calculations of how many she would deal with on average. *It's possible that they have abilities too,* her mind warned.

The guards approached one of the hiding spots. Gwen's spine tingled, her body pulsed with adrenaline as she waited for the exact moment to intervene. Then she saw it; a shoe and pant leg exposed in the light. *How could she be so reckless?* Gwen thought frustrated with Baylee now.

Gwen emerged from the shadows while their backs were turned. "Excuse me sirs, I was wondering if..."

"Not now," the guard signaled to the exposed shoe in the corner.

"It's just a shoe. What's the big deal?" Gwen played the fool's role as she approached them.

Gwen took advantage of her proximity to the guards. *They obviously trust me.* Gwen looked around the room and saw no one. At the speed of light she snaked her hands underneath the guards arms and in a full circle swung them inward, locking out their elbows, and crashing their heads together.

The guards didn't know what hit them. They were unconscious now. Baylee leaped out from the darkness and helped Gwen pull the guards into the darkness making sure none of their clothes were exposed in the light.

"Sweet moves Red," Baylee complimented.

"Why does everyone call me that?"

Baylee gave her a look as if to question her seriousness.

Three guards came rushing from nowhere in high alert. "Hold it right there! We need to see some identification!"

The girls looked at each other then back at the guards. "Relax. What seems to be the problem?"

"We've been seeing a lot of new faces around here this evening."

"We're new here. Are you guys always this paranoid?"

Baylee asked.

"Identification now!" a guard demanded as they cautiously approached.

"Hang on, I know it's in here somewhere," Gwen said digging into her pockets. "Oh no, I think I dropped it," she put her hands up defensively, "let me retrace my steps," Gwen reached into the darkness while the guards focused on Baylee.

"And you?" the guard asked impatiently.

"Yeah sure, no problem." She dug into her pocket knowing she would find nothing.

Gwen removed the badges from the unconscious officers and borrowed the ability she acquired from Rook to change the pictures and information, then quickly sneaked one in Baylee's back pocket as she passed by.

"Here you go," Gwen offered.

As the guard observed Gwen's identification, she eyed Baylee to check her back pocket.

"And you?" the third guard asked more impatient than before.

Baylee dug into her back pocket. "Here it is," she said handing it to the other guard.

"You must keep identification in plain view at all times."

"Have we had trouble in the past?"

"Well, no. But you can never be too sure."

"You sure know how to make a new girl feel welcome," Baylee said sarcastically.

The guards continued back in the opposite direction.

"Two of us remains in the shadows. When the coast is completely clear, I will grab them. I will lead you to the bus. It's still waiting."

"How do you know all of this."

"I just do."

The hunters watched in the distance, as Gwen carried out her plan; moving the wardlows from the facility onto the bus.

"Very interesting," Sythen said.

"Indeed," Junter agreed.

"What is she? Not one of them and not one of us. So what then?" Sythen asked.

"Why does she help them? Why is she concerned with anyone other than her own kind? Perhaps she is one of a kind and seeks to bridge the gap," Sythen suggested.

"Insightful my friend," Junter complimented.

"So why are we letting them all escape again?" Sythen asked.

"Zaleyona thinks this creature is the key to unlocking something far greater than the gift of an occasional form-life. If this creature is of the v-spec, then there is a good chance her group will contain most, if not all, of the other specs required to fill the prism cell. With the prism cell, we can inhabit any form of our choosing, even in this world!"

"Cut out the middle man!" Sythen exclaimed.

"Exactly!" Junter said, pleased with the learning curve of his young apprentice.

"Oh man! I want one of each!" Sythen said excitedly.

"Don't be greedy my friend. We must be patient," Junter attempted to bring his excitement level down a notch. "V-specs are almost impossible to catch. If we blow this, Zaleyona will never let us take form. The hunting thing is alright, but I want to be able to feel the grass in my toes, smell the air with my nose, and feel textures with my bare fingers. I want to experience the things that make them laugh, fall in love, make them cry. I want to feel something."

Chapter Twenty

Gwen used her own memories to navigate the straw field. She could sense the wardlow's paranoia as their feet crunched the straw beneath them. Everyone remained quiet. She took them to the Dresden sanctuary.

Gwen used the gift she acquired from Rook to open the stone structure. When the door opened she almost fainted. She gasped loudly as her heart began pounding harder in her chest.

"Rook! You're here!"

"I said I would be." He looked at her confused.

"Well, come on in already. How did you get here in the dark?" Rook asked confused. "Did you figure out how to use the sun lens?"

Gwen gave a hesitant perplexed look. "It turns out that I have more abilities than I thought. I'd rather talk about that another time. Sun lens?" Her perplexed look deepened.

"The black mirror. I found the paperwork on it. It's a project Alexa calls Sun Lens. Her research team developed it. You can see through it," Rook smiled excitedly before continuing. "In the sunshade!"

"Like sunglasses of my world," Gwen said almost under her breath. "That knowledge would have come in handy a little earlier," Gwen said aloud slightly irritated.

"Hey. I didn't know. I stumbled across it at the house before coming here to meet you."

The wardlows observed the room in awe, grateful to have their sight back.

"Wow. This place is amazing!" Marr said.

Gwen looked around the room and noticed Baylee was missing. "Are we missing someone?"

The wardlows looked at each other and back at her with confused expressions.

"Someone is missing!" *She was definitely on the bus with the rest of us. Did she get lost in the straw? Is anyone else missing?* Gwen wondered for a moment. "You guys stay here. I need to check something out."

"Hey. Thanks for everything you've done tonight," a man said.

"Yeah. We would have been doomed without you," a woman agreed.

"The battle is far from over. I don't know what we are up against next," Gwen warned.

"Well then, I guess we'd better enjoy freedom while it lasts," the woman said.

"If I'm not back tonight..." Gwen said.

"The sun has been up for far too long. None of us have much longer tonight," the man said.

"Yeah. We are lucky to have made it this far without collapsing," Marr agreed.

"Is that what happens?" Gwen asked astounded.

"Once a body is drained it collapses. You had better hope to be lying in the sunshade if it happens. You drain yourself completely with no source to recharge, you die. Very simple," Marr explained.

"How long can one go without sunshade and/or sleep?"

"Three days without sunshade, with plenty of sleep, but only 20 hours maximum without sleep."

"Sunshade or no sunshade," a wardlow added. "Sleep trumps sunshade."

"I must check the fields for missing wardlows. I know there were more of you when we left the bus."

"A good opportunity to try out the sun lens." Rook

said confidently. Gwen thought he sounded oddly at ease under the circumstances. He was, without a doubt, an accessory to a major crime now."

"So, you're not mad at me anymore?" Gwen asked hopeful.

Rook approached her calmly. "No I'm not. I'm relieved you're safe and I intend to do everything in my power to keep you that way." Gwen hugged him. The wardlows watched silently in disbelief.

"I need to get out to the field to look for Baylee before too much time passes."

"Are you sure you want to go out there by yourself?" Rook asked protectively. He couldn't help but wonder if Baylee was a delusion all along. Gwen had been through enormous stress today.

"It's for the best. Someone needs to look after these guys while I'm gone. If anything happens to me, it is essential to keep them safe. You can't allow them to fall into the hands of the hunters. It's the only way to keep Raven safe long enough to figure out a way to rescue her."

"This feels like good-bye. I don't like it," Rook pleaded.

"Not goodbye—see you later," Gwen said.

"Not too much later. The wardlows are right. You don't have much time. I wish you would reconsider. Go in the morning."

"I can't. I won't lose Baylee again. Besides, if one of us is caught, we all get caught. I sense the presence of hunters. This is something I have to do."

Rook embraced her one last time. "Please hurry. It kills me that I can't protect you. You are my only hope of saving Raven. I can't do it alone."

His embrace felt firm and permanent. Gwen's center swirled within—her emotions swirled alongside logic; individual insoluble solutions, twirling in tandem like a snake biting it's own tail.

With the door opened, Gwen reached for the sun lens. Holding the black disc at eye level she was astounded by what she saw. "Amazing!" The disc was like a peep-hole through the veil of impenetrable darkness; as clear as day.

Rook looked over her shoulder through the lens. "Wow! You should be back in no time!"

"I'm going to back-track through the straw and that's it. Should be in and out of there pronto."

Visually sweeping the park with her perfectly clear day-vision tool she saw no one. Gwen sensed the hunters presence but didn't let it worry her. *Let them come. I will defeat them single-handedly.* The instincts of the large jungle-cat pumped through her veins. The thought of the fight thrilled her. Something she didn't understand but refused to question. It felt good; superhuman. She suddenly felt like she were the hunter on the prowl for its prey. The adrenaline was invigorating.

The increase in adrenaline drained on her consciousness. Suddenly overcome by a falling sensation, gravity increased exponentially against her body. Another familiar sensation; being sucked into the ground helplessly —only this time—she wasn't standing but lying. No longer able to look through the sun lens, darkness paralyzed her. She was suddenly disoriented by sensations beyond her control.

The falling sensation subsided. Cold shivers passed through her body. She opened her eyes to find herself in a dimly lit snowy landscape. Not as cold as the snow of her native world but much colder than the 72 degrees she grew accustom to in Alexa's world. Snowflakes fell from the gray sky at an alarming rate. No footprints in sight. She began to assess her own feet. "What the...?"

Her body barely recognizable; replaced by a translucent purple hue. "Am I dead?" Gwen wondered aloud.

"No." A female voice answered from beside her.

Gwen's perspective changed without turning her head to the voice beside her where Baylee stood in the form she recognized.

"Baylee! What's happening?"

"You are between the layers of the world."

"Me? What about you? You no longer stand in my world. You died!"

"Energy is never destroyed, only transfered. I evolved; moved on. It's beyond your comprehension. Your perspective is limited—as it should be. These worlds are not separate. They are simply layers of the same world."

"Why am I here? How did I get here?"

"Follow me. I will guide you safely," Baylee assured.

Gwen trekked through the snow with her best friend confused and unsuspecting. No tracks appeared on the snowy surface as they moved forward. A single tree appeared in the distance; leafless and covered in ice. The vast branches shimmered despite the dark atmosphere.

"Because you see nothing does not mean there is nothing to see," Raven had said. *She said I brought them to the desert land. Did I bring us here?*

"What's the matter?" Baylee asked concerned.

Gwen felt a speed-bump; a hiccup in her soul center causing an eerie, crawly sensation up her formless spine. Her stride stopped abruptly; instinctively, she induced the calm—right then and there—her mind flooded with thousands of images moving at the speed of light. A loud shrieking noise broke her concentration. When her eyes snapped open she was no longer in the snowy landscape. She was standing formlessly before the edge of a large black void in the ground. The sky full of black and gray clouds whirled overhead. Lightening streaked across the sky in constant intervals.

The shrieking sound came from the gray and black shadow beside her. The shadowy semi-formless figure no longer resembled her best friend but a sharp-featured woman with scary angry eyes; like solid shiny chrome spheres and medium-length, black, curly hair.

The semi-formless woman suddenly lunged toward Gwen. Overcome by a sudden wave of heat Gwen stood tall against the intruding figure. Gwen heard a low buzzing sound like pulsing electricity as she snapped her chest and abdomen forward. The invisible shock-wave of heat expanded like a compressed spring, blasting her opponent through the air and onto her back.

"You will not get away from me! I have your body, the woman shrieked."

"If that were true you wouldn't be trying to lure me across the dark void!" Gwen shouted angrily. "You have a useless shell. You need the nut inside and you don't have to tools to crack it." Gwen taunted.

"I am one step closer and there is no way you can stop me. Once you return home, you will be powerless and fragile. Go ahead, turn back. Make this easier for me." Her eyelids squinted hard against her solid chrome eyes.

Gwen turned away and let the calm engulf her senses.

Rook worried for Gwen as she closed the door behind her. His center twisted with concern. *Gwen is strong. She knows what she's doing.*

"So, anyone care to tell me what happened tonight?" Rook asked in an upbeat sounding mood.

Marr was the most carefree, also the youngest of the wardlows. He was grateful to be free and enthusiastic about the journey ahead. He felt good about his role in the rescue. "She rescued us. It was awesome!"

The other wardlows turned to look at Marr disapproving of his thrilled tone.

"That's amazing but how?"

The wardlows took turns telling Rook their side of the story. Rook felt as though he loved her more than ever and wished he had never doubted her in the first place. He thought the argument might have been a good thing. *All things happen for a reason.* Despite all that has happened he firmly believed that.

"Are you one of us?" Marr asked.

"A wardlow? No. I'm just a regular guy."

The wardlows gasped in amazement.

"Gwen and I are-uh married," he said scratching a twitchy nerve on the back of his head.

Their jaws dropped leaving them speechless.

"She has been gone a long time. I'm getting worried. I wish I would have held onto the sun lens or gone with her."

"I have night-vision, I will go look for her," Marr volunteered.

"It might be dangerous out there." Rook sounded

219

concerned for the young boy.

"It's the least I can do. She put her life on the line for all of us tonight. It wouldn't be right for me to stay here when I might be able to help," Marr argued.

"Okay, but make it quick. If you find her or not, come back here within a few minutes," Rook lectured like a protective big brother.

"Don't worry. I plan to spend as little time away from the pack as possible," Marr assured Rook.

Keeping his promise Marr returned in five minutes. Rook opened the door hoping to see Gwen and Marr both safely appear from the darkness.

Marr stepped in and closed the door behind him. "She's gone."

Rook felt the ice pour from his center into his arms. "Did you check the entrance?"

"I ran as fast as I could. I called for her but she never answered. There is no trace of her."

Rook backed up and sat against the marble table. "I knew I shouldn't have let her go out there alone!"

The wardlows kept to themselves.

"What do we do now?" Marr asked worried.

"We sleep and wait until morning. What else can we do?" Rook asked sounding defeated. "There isn't enough sunshade inside for all of us to sleep under. We can take turns sleeping on the platform throughout the evening. Unless anyone feels comfortable about rolling themselves out the door and onto the grass," Rook suggested suppressing a chuckle.

"I think I can go one night without sunshade. I just need to get some sleep," Marr said.

The other wardlows agreed. One night without sunshade would be no big deal.

"Suit yourself. I will take the platform then. If any of you change your mind, just let me know. We'll sort this all out in the morning," Rook assured them.

Just as they were discussing Gwen's disappearance hopelessly, the locks on the door churned loudly. Everyone in the room felt their heart fall from the delicate placement in their chests. Gwen fell against the door before her body slammed onto the floor. Rook went to his feet and to her side before he knew he was even standing. He scooped her body into his lap and held her shoulders against his arm, her hair flowing over-top. His heart beating hard in his chest and in his throat. "Gwen!" He shook her gently a few times feeling breathless with every passing split second. "No, no, no—come back to me. Everything is going to be okay. I will protect you." Rook's hands were trembling. "Please. I won't fail. I can't fail. You're all I have left! Don't leave me." His eyes felt hot and his vision began to blur.

Gwen's eyes fluttered before opening half way. "Rook." Her breathing visibly becoming shallower. "I love you," she breathed again. "Orbondwar."

Rook chuckled humorlessly. A tear squirt out of each eye when he spoke. "Orbondwar always." He was unconsciously rocking her gently. His mind unable to hold onto one coherent thought.

"Baylee...," she breathed.

"Don't worry about her right now. We will find her."

Gwen's eyes and forehead crumpled together and used up most of the energy she had left. "Don't... trusss..."

Rook shushed her. "We can discuss this tomorrow. You need sleep."

"Kiss... me..."

This demand he couldn't refuse. It felt like forever since their last embrace. He adapted to her worldly affections as easily as any native of her world. He felt no shame from his unfamiliar audience. As far as Rook and Gwen were concerned, they were alone in the world in this moment. The heat of her breath and sweetness of her lips were as refreshing as a warm breeze in the flowering orchard. He held her tightly as if afraid she would fall away in his arms like a crumbling sand castle. His firm grip and passionate kiss was not enough to keep her in his world. He felt her body become heavy in his arms. Her lips stood still before her head fell heavy against his arm. He pulled her in close to his body again heavy and limp against his grip. Tears rolled from his eyes into her fiery red hair. Strands clung to his face. The sound of her heartbeat slowed in his ears as her breathing almost ceased to exist. None among the group dared to disturb him. They all sat silently in awe at what they saw, temporarily setting their own concerns aside.

Mimic sat next to the hospital bed, holding her hand in both of his thumbs; gently rubbing the tops of her hand. "I'm so sorry Gwen. I didn't know. I just wanted to surprise you."

Gwen heard the muffled voice somewhere in the distance as she slowly drifted into consciousness. It wasn't the voice she expected to hear. Her eyes pried open and she saw his face with guilt written all over it. His eyes sleep deprived and red from evaporated tears. *This is a familiar scene. Ironic.*

"Nurse! Sh—she's awake! Mimic yelled stuttering for the first time in years.

Gwen was suddenly deeply agitated by the irony. "What's going on? What happened?"

Mimic's excited expression of her waking was now

diluted by guilt, "I uh..." he took a minute to slow his thoughts so he could speak without stumbling, "I didn't know you were allergic to strawberries."

I didn't either, she thought.

"I tried to surprise you with one of my specialty desserts," he paused again, "The reaction wasn't what I expected, and unfortunately, isn't one I will ever forget. So, it's my fault you're in here."

"How long have I been here?"

"A few days."

"For an allergic reaction. Why?"

Mimic rubbed her hand more intensely debating whether or not to go into details. "Well, you were sort-of delusional while you were seizing. You weren't making any sense."

"Do you remember anything I said?" Gwen asked. The heart monitor registered her speeding heart rate.

"We'll talk about it later. You need to rest right now," he said while keeping his eyes on the monitor. "All will be fine. Please try to relax. I miss seeing you conscious."

The change was disorienting but she wasn't tired. Three days of sleep made sure of that. "My memory is a little fuzzy so you'll pardon me if I ask stupid questions for a while. Right?"

"Of course." He got up to kiss her on the forehead. "I'm just so glad you are alright!"

Yeah. I'm fine. A little crazy but otherwise I'm fine. The longer she kept her eyes open, the longer her time as Alexa felt like a crazy dream, or good old-fashioned delusion.

The nurse came in. "Good morning. Your grandma will be glad to see you are awake. She is exhausted with worry. I argued with her to go home and rest. She has been under too much stress lately. I assured her you would be fine."

Another nurse came in behind her with a syringe in-hand; light blue fluid inside. "This will make you sleepy," he said injecting the substance intravenously. Within five seconds she felt heavy; 10 seconds, her senses drifted off. Just prior to losing consciousness she caught a glimpse of a painting on the table at the foot of her bed. *Weeping for Raven?*

Epilogue

Bev didn't argue with the nurse. She knew there was no need to stay at the hospital for an allergic reaction. It didn't make sense though; Gwen suddenly developing a reaction to strawberries. *I hope they weren't doing anything stupid; like drugs or that cough syrup thing I heard about on the news. Kids these days,* she thought.

Bev didn't know what she expected to find in Gwen's bedroom. She had to remind herself she wasn't snooping and that she trusted Penguin. *Parents do these things when they worry.* Her intuition led her to the nightstand drawer where she found a journal. "She won't mind if I take a peak," Bev justified. "I just want to see if she is still writing letters to Baylee. I won't read it, I just want to take a quick peak." Bev told herself. Her heart raced as she reached for the journal.

Bev's guilt was quickly replaced with concern. She expected to find confessions of her admiration for Mimic or how her first days as a college student were. She couldn't stop reading the journal as she promised herself she would. The topics of the journal reminded her of Madison. *Oh Dear! It's like a recurring nightmare. She's been acting so normal. It doesn't make any sense. Maybe this time we will catch it early. If Ben finds out, he will lose it.* Bev decided that she would keep this secret. Just until Ben fully recovers from his panic attack.

"Well I guess they aren't coming," Cat finally said aloud. "I think she's going to try and do this on her own. What now?" she sighed.

The group remained quiet and fidgety for another moment before Jazz spoke, "What if something happened to them?" Jazz's tone saturated with genuine concern.

"Well then I guess it's only a matter of time before our location is blown," Hui-ming responded; sounding selfish; feeling defeated. "Hence the reason for our secret location," he added sarcastically.

"We could always try calling," Brendon suggested.

"You know we can't do that now," Hui-ming said, "if she has been captured, they could set a trap to find us."

Jazz glared at Hui-ming, "If she has been caught, they will find us via her memories anyway. We can't abandon the mission without knowing for sure what has happened!"

Hui-ming was frustrated with all of them now, "We are not abandoning the mission. We are following protocol. Alexa specifically ordered this. Why do I always have to be the bad guy?"

"Let's take a drive past Alexa's house and see if Rook's car is there," Pico suggested.

Cat stood up, "I'll go with you. *I'm* not afraid," she said while snubbing the others.

"I'm not afraid," Jazz replied, "I'm with you two. Why don't *you,* Jazz said eying Hui-ming and Brendon, think of a plan while we check out the area? We'll respond 111 if we find them and 0 if we don't." Jazz commanded. "If it's a 0, we meet at the second location."

"I'm not scared but I'm not crazy either," Hui-ming answered.

The door at the top of the stairs slammed shut before he could close his mouth.

Gwen's dreams were confusing; images of so many different faces and events shuffled in front of her eyes. She felt as if she were spinning. The shuffling stopped and she saw the back of a curly-haired red-head, small-framed woman, facing away from her.

Gwen's image spun in a slow 360 and the other girl's face came into view. As the circle spun a quarter clockwise, she saw the girl was staring straight ahead, oblivious to Gwen's intent stare. Gwen saw the mirror out of her left periphery. The girl was staring at herself in the mirror but the reflection didn't match. Gwen thought she saw her own face in the mirror but didn't have enough time to observe further before the circle arched another quarter clockwise.

Gwen was suddenly behind the mirror. The mirror's backside began to ripple and turn transparent. The rippling slowed and she saw the girl staring her straight in the face. Gwen put her palm to the watery image, a solid sheet of glass beneath her grip. A taller figure approached the girl from behind and wrapped his arms around her waist. Gwen's heart broke, and her fists tightened, at the sight of them together. She knocked on the watery glass and called for him, "Rook! I'm here!" Her words were thin and muffled by the thick, watery glass. It was obvious that they couldn't hear nor see her. The red-head's perfect lips arched into a smile as she closed her eyes and sighed at the loving touch of her husband. Gwen used both of her hands to pound on the glass, but it made no sound. She tried to scream but made no sound. The more she panicked, the less control she had.

Gwen sat up in the hospital bed as quickly as her weak human body would allow. Soaked with sweat, her heart pounded against her rib cage as if she had just run a marathon. Mimic panicked as a nurse rushed to check on her.

"What's happening! Is she okay?" Mimic was standing but didn't remember doing so.

The nurse quickly gauged Gwen's vital signs. "Panic attack," the nurse said relieved. "It was just a bad dream. You will be fine. Take a few deep breaths. You're friend is here with you," the nurse reassured her. "This will pass within minutes. Don't worry," the nurse told Mimic. "I will be back to check on her shortly."

"That painting... how did it get here?" Gwen asked confused.

"I set it there for you. Instead of bringing flowers, I brought you a painting of a flower."

"Where did you get it?" Gwen asked curiously.

"I painted it a few years back."

"*You* painted it?"

"Yeah. Is that hard to believe?" Mimic asked defensively.

"It's just that-I swear I saw it somewhere before. It looks so familiar."

Mimic was insulted by her remark. "I painted it right out of my own mind! It's not a rip off! Actually, It's my most proud work."

"Relax. I didn't mean anything by it. I really like it."

"I call it Weeping Raven Rose," Mimic said.

"Catchy. You are so artistic. I think you could make a good living with your artwork," Gwen complimented hoping she could soothe his bruised ego.

"What inspired you to paint it? Purple and black is my favorite color combination you know."

"I sort of figured that out. I'm not really sure how the idea came about. I wanted to paint something simple. As the layers unfolded I saw the raven in the rose. I thought it was a cool optical illusion so I kept the bird outline in mind as I continued painting the rose."

Mimic scooted his chair closer to the bedside so he could hold her hand. Gwen was reluctant to hold his hand but didn't want to be rude. As Gwen's breathing slowed to normal, the images in her mind slowed too. Mimic's hand was warm on her clammy cold hand but he didn't seem to mind. The warmth from his hand flowed through her arm, across her shoulders and branched out throughout her body in a soothing current of relief. A memory began to surface.

"You kissed me!" Gwen said suddenly astounded by the memory.

Mimic's hand squeezed hers a little tighter than before and his cheeks began to flush pink. "I thought you might have forgotten that part," he said sounding embarrassed.

Gwen's memory flooded with feelings for Mimic. Suddenly she was overcome by them. She felt as if she missed him so much that it was impossible. *These feelings are real! Did any of this really happen?* Gwen began to question her sanity but felt those questions could wait. *Right now, I just want to go home.*

"I do remember now," Gwen said.

"I'm sorry about that. I know you said you just wanted to be friends," Mimic began explaining.

"I don't remember saying that," Gwen admitted. "You aren't the one who should be sorry. I'm sorry for ruining the moment," Gwen said.

"It was definitely a moment to remember." Mimic rolled his eyes at the memory, "me and my bad timing," he added.

"I think the timing was perfect. It's a unique story," Gwen reassured.

"Not one to brag about. That's for sure," Mimic said overcome with shame.

"The kiss of death. I think it's a pretty sweet story," Gwen admitted.

"Why doesn't that surprise me?" Mimic asked sarcastically.

"Practice makes perfect," Gwen suggested.

"True. You proved that on your last math exam. You're lucky you were allowed to retake it you know?"

"Would you just kiss me already. Geez! You are killing me here."

This kiss was one they wouldn't forget. It may not have been the most romantic backdrop but neither one of them were really aware of their surroundings anyway. In this moment, Gwen didn't have a care in the world—not about Rook, wardlows, the mission, Baylee, or her grandparents. This was *her* moment and she was going to indulge selfishly without regret.

CPSIA information can be obtained at www.ICGtesting.com
Printed in the USA
LVOW060010120911

245825LV00003B/5/P